PLEASURE TO THE MAX!
Cami Dalton

HARLEQUIN®

TORONTO • NEW YORK • LONDON
AMSTERDAM • PARIS • SYDNEY • HAMBURG
STOCKHOLM • ATHENS • TOKYO • MILAN • MADRID
PRAGUE • WARSAW • BUDAPEST • AUCKLAND

ISBN-13: 978-0-373-79418-8
ISBN-10: 0-373-79418-5

PLEASURE TO THE MAX!

This edition published by arrangement with Harlequin Books S.A.

® and TM are trademarks of the publisher. Trademarks indicated with ® are registered in the United States Patent and Trademark Office, the Canadian Trade Marks Office and in other countries.

www.eHarlequin.com

Printed in U.S.A.

Prologue

Russian countryside, 1920

THE KING OF THE GYPSIES, Rajko Sanderzej, stared up at his bound hands and cursed under his breath as a drop of sweat dripped down the center of his naked chest. Of course, his entire body was naked. Naked and aroused. Give a female the ability to fulfill her every sexual fantasy and this was what happened…pure erotic torture.

"You look good like that," Stasi said, her voice with an undertone that made the muscles in his stomach pull tight.

Rajko smirked, afraid that if he spoke he'd give away just how affected he was by her shocking new game. His wrists were secured by a length of rope that had been looped over one of the thick wooden beams that ran above his head, just below the ceiling of the abandoned cottage. He didn't bother struggling to get loose. There was no point. There were powers at work far stronger than the tether that held him. Not to mention that he was too busy suffering through the most painful erection of his life.

He'd never been more excited. Either Rajko had a secret submissive streak, which he highly doubted, or the thought of his once shy and wounded lover turned bold tigress of domination had him twitching with lust.

Frankly, he should be annoyed rather than fighting not to spill his seed on the scuffed wooden floor before she even touched him. He was the recognized Rom Baro of the Gypsies, the leader of his band of people. He was the only Romani male ever to have been born with the gift of second sight and the ability to cast and quicken charms.

He'd kept his clan safe and fed through a world war, then led them across Russia in the midst of a revolution. His skill with a knife was unparalleled, and both his looks and prowess brought him any woman he wanted whether Gypsy or *gadje*.

Yet here he stood, twisting like a convict from the gallows, all at the whim of a mere slip of a girl who'd wound her way around his heart and whom he loved above all others. Or, rather, more like a sex slave bound and ready to perform his mistress's bidding. Oh, yes, with her newfound inner vixen, his Stasi would definitely prefer the latter comparison.

The little hellion trailed her hand over his hip and down his flank as she circled behind him then around to the front. Rajko rocked forward on the balls of his feet, his cock thrust brutally in the air. He swallowed, clenching his hands into fists. While he scrambled for an ounce of control, he could do no more than stare; Stasi's entire form was backlit by the fire. She'd started a blaze in the hearth to take off the early spring chill, and the flames crackled invitingly.

Her brown hair tumbled loosely down her back, and she was as bare as he except for the black silk scarf knotted sideways at her hip. The scrap hid nothing, merely accentuating her curving buttocks and the ruffle of curls at the meeting of her thighs. The tiny gold key that she wore around her neck glittered tauntingly. Just thinking about the kind of power she held, and what the key symbolized, made his blood pump in dark, thick pulses. She was only a step away. The small distance was killing him.

His breath slipped out. "You are so beautiful, my Krasili."

She placed her fingers against his lips, then jerked her head to look at the window over her shoulder, apparently to make sure the shutters were closed tight. They were, along with the only door.

"You shouldn't call me that," she said in quiet urgency. "What if someone heard."

Voice dry, he responded, "I'm standing here strung up like a gutted deer. I'm far more concerned about what someone could see rather than hear. Besides, in my eyes, you are a princess. My princess," he said, referring to the Gypsy term he'd just spoken. He shrugged his shoulders as much as the rope would allow. "It's just a word. Your reaction is what would trigger suspicion. Besides," he soothed, "you are safe. No one can hurt you now, and I will keep your secrets hidden."

Her cheeks going pink, she ducked her chin, then rose up on her toes to press her forehead into the curve of his chest. Her breasts molded to his torso. His flesh burned, and he shivered. The flickering light played over her skin, turning the scars that marred her back and torso silvery.

This time he did pull against his bonds, his arms aching to hold her. She'd come so close to dying. It had been almost two years since he'd found her, broken and bleeding on the forest floor in the midst of a revolution-torn Russia.

She'd been barely conscious, blood soaking her dress from a dozen wounds. On the cusp of womanhood, her wealth and nobility of great fame in the area, he'd recognized her immediately and known that those who'd attacked her would seek her out to finish their evil work. If for no other reason than to claim the czar's ransom of jewels with which she'd escaped, and that had glimmered from the torn lining of her clothes. Shushing her frightened whimpers, he'd gathered her into his arms and taken her back to his people.

Remembering that time, Rajko nuzzled the top of her head, smiling into her hair. Living and caring for his wounded angel, his feelings had grown beyond what he'd ever thought himself capable. But after her attack she'd become almost fearful, her demeanor quiet and shy. Trying to get more than the most timid of smiles from her had been a daily battle. Though his little mouse had furtively been every bit as fascinated by him, her eyes constantly following him around their camp.

Night after night he'd watch the beautiful young woman, who called herself Stasi, across the campfire as she wrote out her thoughts and secrets in a small diary. And, Rajko had believed, she wrote of her love and desire for him, knowing in his soul that she was a woman of deep hidden passions.

Hoping to win her heart, and release the pain that had crippled her with fear, he'd carved for her a lover's box and placed it under one of the Gypsies' most rare and potent charms. About the size of a cigar case, a lover's box had become a popular trinket among the young *gadje* women who kept love letters or a journal filled with amorous yearnings for their beaux locked inside. The key was worn as a charm on a bracelet or necklace, a seductive symbol to any male by whom it was seen.

He'd designed the powerful spell so that whenever Stasi wrote her sexual longings and fantasies in her diary, she had only to lock the slim book inside the lover's box and they would come true for her with the man she desired…none other, of course, than Rajko himself.

At the thought of just how well his gift had worked, his mouth slowly curved into what he had no doubt was an unholy grin and he chuckled wickedly.

Stasi lifted her head, and studied his amusement. She nipped his chin with her pearly little teeth. "Hmm, in my fantasy you were begging, not laughing," she said. "I'll have to do something about that."

Rajko grunted. "I think you've done more than enough, Krasili."

Stasi ran the curves of her nails down the inside of his raised arms, over his chest and down to the muscles that ran on each side of his lower stomach in a diagonal arrow to his groin. The air in his lungs hissed out in a rush.

Clearly fighting a smile, she assured, "You're just upset at how you arrived. Next time I decide to write out my bondage dreams, I'll be quite specific in the details," she said, referring to the idiosyncrasies of the lover's box.

Yes, the spell he'd created did indeed make her fantasies come true. This, however, left far too many options for fate to play with while getting all the key players into place. And fate seemed to enjoy riling up as much mischief and mayhem as possible along the way. There were times that, in spite of the spine-wringing benefits, Rajko wished she'd grow tired of his wildly successful gift and be happy to hide it away until some other poor woman needed its secrets.

"Next time you should try doing it the old-fashioned way. In a bed. Me on top. No frills. Just the basics. You don't know. You might like it."

Now it was her laugh that sounded wicked, and she slid to her knees before him. She laid her cheek against his thigh and her breath washed across him, stirring the dense hair at the base of his length.

"Oh, I don't think so, my beautiful Gypsy king," she said, pausing to give the skin between his groin and thigh a slow lick. He actually growled before cutting off the harsh noise escaping his throat. Her palms fit perfectly along the flat planes at the sides of his buttocks, rubbing and pressing, while her lips slipped beneath his heavy stones. She opened her warm, wet mouth impossibly wide then gently sucked as much of him in as she could take. He could hear her lips and tongue erotically working him, and he squeezed his eyes shut and dropped back his head.

His heart banged against his ribs. He had to swallow twice before he finally found his voice and asked, "Why not?"

As her small fist worked its way between his thighs and she pressed two fingertips to the smooth skin behind his sack, her lips loosened their hold on his flesh, though they still touched and brushed against him as she said, "Because we have the kind of passion that legends are made of."

And with his gift of second sight, Rajko knew she was right and could only hope that the next poor man who found himself at the mercy of the lover's box understood its true value and discovered the ultimate secret within…that the magic of fulfilling a woman's desires was the only treasure worth having….

1

St. Petersburg, Russia, Present Day

MINERVA PARKER had done many things in her eighty years of life, but flat-out stealing a rather mediocre, inexpensive antiquity had not been one of them—until today. And damn if her theft of a few minutes ago hadn't been pure, glorious fun. The last time she could remember enjoying herself as much had been decades ago during an excavation in Cairo when she'd fought off a group of bandits who'd tried to rob a grave she'd uncovered, with nothing more to defend herself than her twenty-two caliber and a whip.

Minerva was a treasure hunter, and had been for the past fifty years. In other words, long before Lara Croft had ever dreamed of raiding her first tomb, Minerva had been on the scene, chasing relics and getting herself into the sort of hair-raising adventures that would make the fictitious video game character's exploits seem downright subdued.

Smiling to herself, though she made sure to make the expression suitably vacant and dotty, Minerva casually entered the lobby of one of the finest hotels in St. Petersburg, then crossed to the elevator and stepped inside. She didn't bother to check behind her to see if she was being followed. No one paid attention to old people and she'd just left the legitimate owner of her ill-gotten gains, Max Stone, none the wiser to the robbery and enjoying a drink at the Czar's Club, a seedy bar in downtown St. Petersburg.

Really, it was far too easy. Slip on a pair of reading glasses and hunch her shoulders a bit to give the appearance of being stooped with age, and people either completely ignored her or looked at her as if she'd just had her ticket punched for a one-way ride on the Alzheimer's express. However, she was quite disappointed in Max. They might not exactly travel in the same circles, but, as the saying went, it was a small world out there and the antiquities community was no different. After running in to her since he was a rascally teen accompanying his father—a professor in archeology—from dig to dig, the ridiculously handsome scoundrel should have known better.

She was a force to be reckoned with at any age and those who forgot did so at their own peril. Of course he'd been understandably distracted by a seemingly unimportant curio, one of the many second-rate artifacts that a small-time Russian fence had been trying to hawk to him and the other hunters thronging the Czar's Club. A quite normal occurrence for this time of year.

Every summer the International Antiquities League, or IAL, held a conference here in St. Petersburg.

Though the weeklong convention brought together the leading experts from various universities and museums around the world, they weren't the only ones to take over the picturesque city.

The symposium also attracted every student with enough euros to nab a rail pass, every private collector, treasure hunter—or, as some preferred, antiquities hunter—black market merchant, and hobbyist who wanted to play Indiana Jones. And a person in the know could learn just as much in the Czar's Club, where the more nefarious members of the above list congregated, as she could in any lecture hall.

Which is why Minerva herself had been in the establishment, drinking a glass or two of vodka—freezing cold, no ice. She might be eighty, but she wasn't out of the game yet or about to miss all the action by going to bed early. Tonight, however, when she'd walked into the bar and gotten a feel of the room, she'd had the distinct impression that it would be better to slip into the background, watching and listening rather than charging into the action. From there, playing the little-old-lady card had been a no-brainer and had, as usual, worked like a charm.

Minerva entered her suite, then moved to the sitting area, shrugging her large tote bag off her shoulder and onto the coffee table. Sinking into the feather pillows on the settee, she smiled as she pictured the look on Max's face when he realized that he'd been robbed blind.

Of course, just picturing Max's masculinely beautiful face would be enough to make any woman smile, and she was no exception. Two or three inches over six feet, he had piercing blue-green eyes, *the* body for a man to have and the most unusual hair. Quite stunning, actually, with streaks of color from mink-brown to shining gold running through the too-long mass.

Yet Max Stone was more than handsome. He was dangerous and unpredictable. A scoundrel to the bone. His personality and presence were a combination of Han Solo meets Rhett Butler, crossed with that nefarious Sawyer character from the television show *Lost,* all rolled into one magnificent package.

Minerva had once had a lover like him and she almost sighed aloud at the memory. Every woman should have a thrilling and passionate love affair with an unrepentant rogue like Max Stone. Each moment in their company was exciting and they could usually back up their potent appeal with masterful expertise in the bedroom.

Nothing at all like the spineless idiots her beautiful young great-niece, Cassie, somehow managed to get herself wrapped up with. Especially the toad—as Minerva liked to call him—to whom Cassie had been engaged. Fortunately, the toad had broken it off all by himself before Minerva had been forced to do something drastic, such as have Cassie kidnapped and deprogrammed.

Sadly, though the young woman whom Minerva loved more like a granddaughter than a distant niece certainly tried to live up to the Parker legacy, things usually had a way of getting completely out of hand for Cassie. Which is why the blasted girl was back at home in Palm

Shores, Florida, managing Minerva's shop, Den of Antiquities, rather than out living her own adventures. According to Cassie, she was merely taking a break and reassessing what she wanted to do with her life, or some such nonsense. In Minerva's opinion she was just plain hiding.

Minerva chuckled and eyed the items on the coffee table. If she was right, the chain of events that she'd just set into motion would more than launch her beautiful great-niece back into society. Wearing what was no doubt a smug grin, Minerva reached for her satchel and lifted out the fruits of her crime.

She stared down at the lover's box she'd liberated from Max. Opening the lid, she removed the diary inside, skimming through the pages and smiling in approval at some of the more interesting entries before setting it back.

After the other hunters had wandered off in search of better merchandise, unaware of what they'd overlooked as junk and left behind, Minerva had watched from a nearby table as Max Stone had swooped in and bought the lover's box from the Russian fence for less than fifty American dollars. The trinket was gaudily painted and in poor condition, but for those aware of its significance, this hardly decreased its value—a find that maybe fifty hunters and scholars combined would even recognize.

Few people were familiar with the Gypsy folklore and fables of almost ninety years ago surrounding the life of the last great Gypsy king, Rajko Sanderzej. Even fewer knew about the lover's box that Rajko had made for the woman he loved.

One tale claimed that the man who possessed Rajko's box held the secret to a treasure for which czars and kings would die. Another claimed that the woman who possessed Rajko's box held the secret to sexual ecstasies beyond those that only the most passionate of females dreamed.

Of course most historians considered it pure bunk, and even among the Gypsies, the existence of Rajko's box had taken on the status of an urban legend. But, great heavens, it boggled the mind to think about the possibilities a woman could explore if she had Max Stone and Rajko's lover's box at her disposal.

Ahh, Minerva remembered thinking wickedly to herself as she'd sat in the Czar's Club, what she wouldn't give to be fifty years younger like her niece, Cassie. It had been on the heels of this titillating thought that Minerva had realized the opportunity in front of her was just too darn good to pass up. And, she didn't have a single doubt that Max would chase after the lover's box.

Max needed the box in order to find Rajko's treasure. Though she might not know it, Cassie needed the box to have the sort of glorious sex that thrust a young woman out of hiding and forced her into the open where the stark light of fleshly pleasures illuminated and empowered her soul. Or at the very least gave her great screaming orgasms.

Minerva glanced at her wristwatch. Late, but at a hotel like this one the front desk staff always catered to guests. She needed packaging materials and tape sent up immediately. She walked to the phone and picked up the receiver.

She doubted that Max had yet discovered the theft. He was probably still slamming back the vodkas and riding out the high of knowing he'd found Rajko's box. Quite a feat since, for almost ninety years, no one had been able to conclusively prove its existence, let alone go after its mythical treasure.

Minerva had about twenty-four hours or so before Max pieced two and two together. Just enough time to express-deliver Rajko's box to Palm Shores. And just enough time to lay a trail for Max to follow, and to give Cassie a head start on using the box Rajko had designed for his woman.

Then it was up to Max Stone to decide just how badly he wanted a czar's ransom in treasure. And up to Cassie to decide just how badly she craved pleasure. Pleasure, as the youngsters would say, to the max…

2

CASSIE PARKER could not think of a single sexual fantasy that didn't sound corny or clichéd. Or one that didn't require an immediate crash diet. All of which was a major bummer since, if Aunt Minerva's package that had arrived yesterday and the accompanying letter were to be believed, Cassie had just been given the key to making her most erotic and forbidden fantasies come true.

Ah, well, Cassie had always believed that Murphy's Law had been written expressly for her, so it was no surprise really that with complete sexual fulfillment within her reach, Cassie was either drawing a blank or worrying about whether she'd look too fat in a French maid's costume. It was just her luck that this magical opportunity would arrive after she'd spent the past seven months eating her way through the ugly breakup with her ex-fiancé, Satan. (His mother had named him Ron, but the woman had been way off on that one.)

Twelve extra pounds, and every ounce counted when

one was five feet two inches tall, on top of an already, er, curvy body type tended to play havoc with a girl's vanity. Heck, she didn't even like shopping for bathing suits let alone conjuring up pornographic images where she played the starring role. Well, if she looked on the bright side, a lover's box that guaranteed life-altering nooky, yet with the potential for crippling self-consciousness and outrageous embarrassment on her part, meant that the whole thing was bound to come true and she'd better start writing.

Grinning to herself—hey, it was either smile or cry in the face of cellulite anxiety—Cassie lifted her wine-glass and took a sip. She leaned against the mound of pillows at the head of her bed. Her legs were crossed, and a brand-spanking-new diary rested on her thighs. The blank white pages gleamed up at her brightly.

Earlier, since Cassie had been at the store, anyway, and since her outrageous aunt would merely hound her until she tried out the lover's box, she'd bought the slim journal. After reading Minerva's letter it had seemed to Cassie that her wild and wacky Friday-night plans of eating chocolate chip cookie dough and giving herself a pedicure could only be enhanced by writing out exotic sexual scenarios and locking them inside an antique lover's box that, according to her illustrious great-aunt, was under a Gypsy love charm.

Then the ramifications had sunk in, and the wine had been brought out.

Cassie stared down at the blank page, suddenly feeling more than a bit stupid about the whole thing.

Granted, it wasn't like she'd canceled a date with George Clooney, but what had earlier sounded like a fun way to pass an evening now seemed sort of dorky and desperate. Two adjectives that pretty much summed up her life.

Sighing, she tossed her empty book and pen down next to her on the bed. She picked up the original diary that had come inside the lover's box and had been written by the Gypsy king's lover, and started flipping the pages. For the most part, the woman had signed her entries as Stasi, though toward the end she'd started penning off as Krasili. Since the handwriting matched, this presumably was a nickname, though that was merely a guess.

In any case, good old Stasi had imagination and daring up the wazoo. She might have started out too shy to talk to her Gypsy king, Rajko, but, with the pages all but smoking, it was apparent that as soon as Stasi had gotten the hang of it she'd become a different woman.

Cassie had read Stasi's entire diary, and noting the other woman's transformation from a timid and fairly vanilla lover to a wild temptress of the night had been inspiring to say the least. Or rather, the general concept had been inspiring, rather than the specifics.

Before she'd started dating Ron, Cassie had been the sort of gal who'd really liked sex. Okay, really, really liked sex, and as long as she'd been aroused past her don't-look-at-my-fat-butt stage, she'd been able to swing from the chandeliers with the best of them. No, Cassie thought sourly, from the little she remembered of the act—pre-Ron era—she didn't need inspiration from Stasi's diary to let go of a few hang-ups so she could enjoy doing the wild thing.

Rather, she needed inspiration to change and grow for the times spent out of bed when, no matter what excavation she'd tagged along on, no matter what extreme sport she'd somehow been conned into trying by Minerva, no matter what exotic career she'd pursued in an attempt to live up to the legacy of her treasure-hunting aunt—not to mention, all the other annoyingly adventurous females in their illustrious family—things had consistently gone haywire and Cassie had always come out looking like a boob.

Oh, who was she trying to kid? Post-Ron she was pretty screwed up in the bedroom, too. Her ex-fiancé, through great stealth and passive-aggressive tactics, had turned her into a weight-obsessed mess who could barely glance at herself in the mirror let alone strut up to a guy as if she were Angelina Jolie and ask him back to her place for a little somethin'-somethin'. Although Cassie had high hopes that this would be a condition she'd get over rather quickly if the right man diligently applied himself to the cause.

Lost in her morbid thoughts, Cassie started when her great-aunt's cat, Creature, jumped up onto the bed. He stalked over to the quilts that she'd pushed into a clump down by her feet. His tail had been broken in a fight, and she watched it twitch back and forth in a disjointed pattern. Cassie liked to think of herself as someone who loved animals, but Creature—so named for his lack of resemblance to a normal feline—put a strain on her self-perception.

Since she shared the top floor of the house with her great-aunt, and the shop she managed for Minerva was downstairs, Creature came as part of the deal, and whenever Minerva wasn't around to keep him company he amused himself by biting and scratching Cassie and generally vandalizing the place to show his displeasure.

Creature dug his claws into the bedding, kneading the sharp little devils back and forth as he rhythmically lifted and lowered his patchily furred paws. The vicious beast stared right at her. Well, one of his eyes stared directly into hers, the other wandered to the left with the accompanying eyelid permanently fixed at half-mast. His personality matched his appearance and she could swear he shot her a look that said, "Lady, you might as well just write down the word *intercourse*, plain and simple, in that little diary of yours, because even a Gypsy love charm can only do so much."

Cassie flattened her mouth, but did nothing, not even shooing him off the bed as he snagged and snarled her blankets. She wouldn't dream of going up against the feral brute without a chair and a whip. Besides, despite being destructive and mean, at least he was company.

Eventually growing tired of his game, Creature plopped down and stretched himself out. Call her nuts, but that cat was clearly an alien life form intelligent enough to take over the planet: no animal should be able to convey so much disdain and mockery on his face.

This time, he gazed directly at her diary before he flicked his attention away, obviously bored with such inactivity. Something about the feline's contemptuous expression reminded her of Ron.

Cassie narrowed her eyes and snatched up her pen. She opened her blank diary to the first page. A neurotic, unlucky mess she may be, but she was not about to be dissed by a damn house cat. Ron, the butthead, had been bad enough. She had her pride. She was a Parker. And Parker women lived life to the fullest and took no prisoners. If she needed to come up with a sexual fantasy, then, by golly, she was going to come up with the hottest, steamiest, wildest fantasy that was ever fantasized.

Ink to paper, she started writing. Cassie wanted power. Specifically, she wanted sexual power. She wanted a man to crave her as he had never craved another woman. She wanted him so filled with lust that whenever he saw her all he could think about was getting inside her before he came. A single glance at her and he was stone hard.

Writing furiously, she expounded on the general theme of her irresistible sexual allure, then decided, oh, what the hell, she might as well deal with all her issues in one fell swoop, and her pen was off again. She wanted excitement. She wanted danger. She wanted adventure.

While Minerva and her mother both thrived on the stuff, Cassie had secretly found the concepts annoying and overrated. And, with her track record, who could blame her? Well, Cassie had. Or did. Or whatever. But no more.

She was going to hold her own and be confident no matter what lay ahead. She didn't want to worry about getting hurt, or embarrassing herself, or making stupid mistakes. She was going to be tough. She was going to kick ass. And the whole time she made lesser mortals look like incompetent turkeys, the man in her fantasy was going to be so brutally aroused that he'd screw her brains out every chance he got. Bullets could be whizzing over their heads and he'd want her. She was going to be the ultimate sex object. Albeit, a tough and powerful one.

Cassie gave a lascivious chuckle. She dotted off the final punctuation mark with a dramatic flourish, then lifted her pen in the air, making a voilà gesture. After a moment, though, she sat up straight and frowned, wondering if she got to have any say as to how this paragon of manly prowess would look. The ever-mysterious Stasi had already had the hots for her stud muffin, Rajko, when she'd used the lover's box. Was Cassie allowed to write down her preferences? It wasn't like the darn thing came with an instruction manual.

Then Cassie shrugged—it was her lover's box and her fantasy; she could do what she wanted. All-righty then, she said to herself, what should he look like…? She tapped the pen against her bottom lip as she ran through the possibilities. One thing was a given. He definitely had to be well-endowed behind his zipper. *Thick* and *large* were the two most salient words that came to mind and she quickly jotted them down. *A physique similar to a Calvin Klein underwear model's* would be fabulous, so she added this specification to her list.

A few seconds later she also added the requirement, *so hot he might as well be from a superior race of godlike beings.* There, she thought, that should leave little to chance. Then she paused, and finished with, *and a sexy killer tattoo!*

Cassie could feel a huge smile spread across her face as she placed the diary inside the lover's box and closed the lid. She leaned over and carefully turned the miniature key, leaving it in the lock. She didn't have a charm bracelet or a spare chain. Short of hanging it from the small yet erotic little nipple ring that she'd gotten back when she'd been trying to spice things up with Ron (a cringe-inducing phase of her life when she'd been desperate for a successful relationship and would have pierced her hoo-ha if she'd thought it would have cranked Ron's motor), she'd have to wait until she could buy a ribbon or something.

Though surely it didn't matter if she wore the key or not as long as she locked her diary inside the box, right? Then again, maybe it did. What did she know? Cassie grinned. Decisions, decisions…

Not that she actually believed that the whoopee-making Gypsy charm would work, but it would be a shame if she actually could've gotten laid by a Calvin Klein underwear model look-alike, yet didn't because she'd screwed up over such a minor point.

Then she decided, *Aw, what the heck*. This was supposed to be for laughs so she might as well go for the triple-X gold medal. Surprisingly having fun, she took the diminutive key out of the lock, then walked over to her dresser. She rummaged through her accessories until she found the tiny hoop of thin, fourteen-karat wire hiding among her earrings. She bunched her shirt up under her neck and after a few minutes of fiddling, turned to the mirror and caught sight of the erotic adornment.

Wowzers. Talk about sexy. She flicked the key with the tip of her finger while a delicious tingle spread through her nipple. The tiny weight was an exquisite presence, subtle yet hard to ignore. She smoothed down her shirt. With the fabric on her bra fairly thin, only the barest hint was visible. She felt almost risqué, like she had a fabulous secret. For a girl with nothing but TiVo and snack foods on the horizon for the rest of the weekend, this was not a bad place to be.

Cassie laughed and stepped over to the bed, picking up the lover's box. It was made of wood and ornately carved, the outside intricately painted with gold-leaf swirls and a variety of hues that age couldn't completely diminish. The gaudy thing somehow reminded her of a treasure chest turned inside out with all the jewel-like tones decorating its exterior. Gypsies were said to love bright colors and flashy ornamentation, and it appeared that King Rajko epitomized the stereotype. Not exactly the most tasteful curio or collectible she'd ever seen, but she liked it and thought it added character to her room.

Her mouth curved into a wide grin, and with a bounce in her stride, she set the lover's box onto her bedside table, then put Stasi's diary in one of the stackable, plastic cubbies inside her closet for safekeeping. Wow, she thought, suddenly aware of her considerably elevated mood. Journaling out her deepest sexual longings had been downright cathartic.

Yes, yes, obviously none of that nonsense about her fantasies was going to come true even if she was wearing the sexy key on her breast. Still, not to have a total Dr. Phil moment here, but…by going through the process of recording her secret desires she felt downright empowered. Free, somehow.

Cassie couldn't stop smiling. She even beamed at Creature when he yowled his displeasure at having his nap disturbed. She'd have scratched the little booger's ear if she didn't think he'd take her hand off.

Laughing as if a burden had been lifted from her shoulders, Cassie strolled into the bathroom and started looking through the powders and gels in the cabinet under the counter. She decided to pamper herself, and deserved the treat. Fifteen minutes later, however, she had a moment's hesitation when she found herself generously waxing parts of her body that were only waxed when a girl planned on getting very, very lucky. For a second she feared that subconsciously she somehow believed that the lover's box was going to work.

Then she shrugged this off, and decided that her aggressive, nudist-colony wax job was really just a sign of her positive, proactive thinking and she should be proud of herself for moving on as if there was truly a chance of anyone seeing her naked before the year was out. The touch-up job to her Honey Hotness toenail polish, and the liberal use of the deliciously scented bubble bath were also signs of her healthy mental state. Or so she assured herself as she lounged back in the warm bathwater, her eyes closed, her feet with their newly painted toes propped on the opposite rim, and the saucy little key to the lover's box floating at her nipple.

Her mind, at the moment, seemed incapable of thinking about much besides sex and she indulged herself, playing out a variety of scenarios where an obscenely handsome man licked, fondled, then fabulously screwed her newly waxed and scrubbed body. Then she heard the unmistakable sound of breaking glass. Cassie groaned.

Creature had no doubt sneaked into the shop downstairs. She was not in the mood to deal with his vandalism when she felt this happy and relaxed. She heard another thump float up the stairs and cursed under her breath. Creature was a porker, on top of all his other attributes, but considering that he weighed only thirty pounds, any thump that made its way up to her apartment suggested the vexing animal was wreaking a path of pure destruction.

Water and bubbles dripping down her body, Cassie jumped from the tub, grabbed the closest towel, then padded off to strangle Creature.

MAX STONE HAD NEVER run across a lock he couldn't pick, but when the damn thing was rusted shut there was only so much a man could do. He cast a quick glance around the moonlit backyard, then lifted his elbow and cracked the glass. That done, he took off his shirt, wrapped it around his hand, then pushed the bottom pane out of its frame. The glass chimed in little plinks as it broke against the floor, quieter than if he had just smashed his way through with a rock.

As he slid his arm inside the window, then broke open the latch, Max silently fumed. If he ever again saw that old battle-ax, Minerva Parker, he was going to throttle her. Just thinking about being ripped off by a woman who was eighty if she was a day made him want to knock out a few more windows. Anger, shock and plain old embarrassment made up a large portion of his present state of mind.

Seventy-two hours ago he'd been in St. Petersburg because that's where treasure hunters went during the IAL conference, and because Victor Hofford had planned to attend. Good old Vic had been a boil on Max's backside since Max had been a teenager dragged around the globe in his father's wake and Victor had signed on as the old man's assistant. Victor, of course, had been an amoral kiss-ass even back then, but Max's dad had been unable to see past his appeased vanity and recognize that the grad student who assisted him was a glorified grave robber and smuggler.

Max didn't necessarily have a problem with either of those job titles, but, at the time, he'd been young and hadn't enjoyed being set up to take the fall when Victor inevitably got caught. He might have been only seventeen, and a hell-raising seventeen at that, but if he was going to rob graves, then smuggle what he stole out of the country, he sure as hell wouldn't have left any tracks. A fact he'd proven a couple of years later when he'd taken up the profession himself.

His father had been dead more than a decade, and all that old crap with Victor, who was now a professor— one of those Ivy League, tenured thugs whose ethics were worse than most organized-crime bosses—should have become ancient history. However, Max had his reasons and it was usually in his best interest to keep an eye on the bastard.

Victor was all but a professional nemesis, and he'd thrown Max into the role of archenemy. The guy must have watched every James Bond marathon ever shown on the Spike TV channel. The only thing missing was the fuzzy white cat and the shifty accent. Although, staying current on whatever fresh hell Dr. Evil spent his time stoking wasn't all for Max's own protection. If he'd been the type of person to keep score, which he was, then he was well in the lead for screwing with Victor's finds and generally robbing relics right out from underneath the idiot whenever the opportunity arose. Immature, yes, but fun as hell.

Three nights ago, though, at the Czar's Club, Max had not been in the mood to deal with Victor's crap and had gotten rid of him with a story in the right ear about a Hindu statue that had supposedly surfaced. Complete and utter bullshit, but Vic had fallen for it.

A smart move as it turned out. Because when the

small-time Russian fence had kept shoving his wares in Max's face, Max had caught a glimpse of something that had sent a queer rush of excitement spreading through his gut. One good look at the lover's box and Max had known what he'd found. Ironically, his father had been one of the few people to believe in the Gypsy king's treasure. Which meant that Victor, as dear old dad's one-time right-hand man, would immediately understand its significance if he ever learned of what Max had stumbled across.

Of course, at the time of his discovery, it had been all Max could do to get his mind around the reality that he was the lucky son of a bitch who'd finally found Rajko's box. And that Victor Hofford was off on a wild-goose chase. Unfortunately, it had been this euphoric rush of adrenaline and his false sense of superiority that had led to the mortifying downfall of being swindled by a senior citizen.

The woman was an evil genius. Hell, he'd seen professional cons with less finesse. If he weren't so damned pissed off, he'd be in awe. The whole sham was pure artistry and Max had found himself screwed over and abandoned before he'd even realized she'd gotten to first base. Infuriatingly, when he'd finally tracked Minerva down and accused her of theft (a beyond ironic moment, he admitted) the wily broad had merely waved her hand dismissively and claimed that she had no idea what he was talking about. Worse, she'd stressed that *her* lover's box had already been sent to her antique shop in butt-fun, Florida, and that it was too late because she'd given it to her great-niece as a present.

The type of guys who hung out in the Czar's Club didn't exactly hand out papers of sale or provenance records, and there had been little that Max could do short of calling out the eighty-year-old woman and challenging her to pistols at dawn. He had no idea what she was trying to pull with her niece, but he didn't really care since he planned to steal the damned thing back, find the treasure, then live out the rest of his life on easy street. Maybe a tropical island with two or three local women to keep him company.

And even more disconcerting than being the victim of such a farcical robbery was the strange sensation that he couldn't shake. A niggling itch prickling the back of his neck. As if there was something hazardous waiting for him, but not the kind of peril he was used to facing. Stupid, because nabbing the lover's box should be a no-worries retrieve and run.

But there you had it. The same rush of adrenaline that pulsed through him when he was on a dangerous hunt was right now surging through his nervous system. To Max, hunting relics was a game, the greater the risk the better. He always gambled, occasionally with his life. He preferred it that way. It made him come alive, the thrill real and palpable in a way nothing else could match, when he risked the ultimate price of failure.

Max challenged every damn odd thrown against him. He flipped fate the bird and got off on the rush of walking away unscathed. And, for some reason, right now his instincts were giving him a hit.

A killer grin curved across his face. Max Stone loved this shit....

Feeling cocky and riding the high—hey, anything was better than thinking about Minerva Parker—he silently climbed through the now-open window. He crouched down once he stepped inside, then pulled out his small flashlight and turned on the beam only to find himself face-to-backside with a stuffed water buffalo. That Minerva had such a bizarre item in the middle of her antique store came as no surprise, but when he stepped around the unfortunate animal and came face-to-breasts with something that was not stuffed and definitely alive, he was more than surprised.

Strangely, he wasn't overly concerned that, for all practical purposes, he'd just been caught. If he had to, he could take down the small, curvy bundle of woman in front of him in less than a second and Max found himself praying that he had to. He slowly ran the beam from his flashlight up the smooth, wet legs dripping water onto the oriental carpet beneath her dainty feet, and over the soaked, clinging towel that looked more suited to drying a pair of hands than wrapping itself around an adult's body. But damn if that's not exactly what the lucky little stretch of terry cloth was being forced to do.

And it was doing a damn poor job of it, he was happy to say, since the damp fabric barely hit the very tippy tops of her thighs, and just covered her small, enticing mound. Max's fingers itched to flick it away and see the exact color of those pretty feminine curls that were hidden from his gaze.

His mouth suddenly dry, he slipped the light up over the heart-pounding curve of her tiny belly clearly outlined by the clinging towel. The sight was enough to make him want to fall to his knees and push his tongue against the enticing dent of her belly button. Then he moved the light a little farther up, to the absolute sweetest, plumpest handfuls of breasts for which he'd ever sprung a boner.

Now, Max generally liked all breasts and had never really had a complaint with any pair he'd seen or touched, but the cherry-tipped duo in front of him looked beyond centerfold perfect. He'd found his dream tits and until this very moment, hadn't even known that he'd had this strong a preference.

Quite frankly, if he was even half as stunned by the rest of her, he was afraid he'd shoot off like a teenager on prom night. So far, every inch of her that he could see had suddenly become his absolute favorite: his favorite kind of toes that he liked to lift to his mouth, then kiss and nibble. His favorite sort of legs that he liked to stroke and caress, and feel wrapped around his torso. His favorite sort of belly that he liked to feel cushioned under his body while he rhythmically pressed his stiff cock into its plump softness as he mimicked the motion he'd re-create when he was deep inside her.

And his hands-down, all-time favorite pair of tatas that he liked to squeeze and suckle and bite until just the pressure of those erect little tips against his tongue was enough to make him come.

His instant, painful attraction to her was so strange, and he felt so damn good about it, that if he didn't know better, he could swear that someone had put a spell on him.

Then the woman said, "Oh…my…gosh…"

Max lifted his light to her face and almost dropped the damned thing. His heart started to pound, slamming against his rib cage. He stiffened his spine and willed himself to stand absolutely still, because he'd never wanted to mate with a woman so badly—there was no other word for the sheer lust-craved act he wanted to perform on her delectable body—and if he so much as twitched, he was afraid he'd nail her where she stood.

And then she said in a voice that he swore made a drop leak from his dick, "I can't believe it. It worked…."

3

CASSIE STARED MUTELY at the very embodiment of her fantasy, wondering if she should scream in terror or knock him out before he could escape. Holy... The lover's box really worked.

Yeesh. Even barely able to see him, his looks had her blushing hard enough to pass out. Yes, indeedy, the man certainly fit the *from a superior race of godlike beings* part of her description, and the phrase *Come to Mama*...flitted through Cassie's mind.

This vaguely surprised her since it would be more in character for her to start kicking herself for requesting someone so far out of her league. But she didn't feel like worrying about the sudden silence of the voice inside her head that liked to keep a running monologue of Cassie's faults, her past failures and the deadly combination of the two that seemed to make her constantly repeat them. Besides, the proper response to such masculine beauty brought via Gypsy magic to satisfy her carnal demands was the happy dance. She felt like jumping around the room and singing, "I get to do him, I get to do him." She restrained herself, just barely.

Instead, she took a big gulp of air. She'd sort of forgotten to breathe. She'd also forgotten that she was wearing a towel, and only remembered when she felt it heading south. She wriggled, trying to save the darn thing.

At her movement, the man's eyes went wide and he dropped his light. The room was thrown completely into darkness and the sound of his cursing floated in the air. Now that she couldn't see him, she tried to drag her thoughts back to reality, frantically telling herself that only a complete idiot would believe her stupid fantasy had anything to do with this freakishly attractive burglar. Her brain was having none of it.

She also decided that she couldn't stand here all night. She either needed to call the cops or have sex with him. She also needed to speak, say something, to figure out what the heck was going on.

And then his light came back on, and that's when she noticed that besides possibly being the sexiest man in existence, completely conjured for her own personal enjoyment, he wasn't wearing a shirt. He'd wrapped it around his hand, a few slivers of glass clinging to the fabric.

If she'd been staring at him before, her eyes were now devouring him. Perfection. Pure male perfection. Ripped and cut without any of that pesky body-builder bulk. All right. Who the hell was this guy? If the lover's box had worked, then it was time for him to get busy doing the job he'd been brought here for, chop-chop. If not, then she needed to screw him before he could figure out where the exits were.

Scanning every golden inch of his exposed skin, she suddenly noticed something was missing and before she could stop herself blurted, "You don't have a tattoo." Okay, so she sounded panicked. That's only because she was.

His head jerked back, and he said, "I beg your pardon?"

"A tattoo. I can't see one." Cassie felt like a complete yahoo but if Adonis here didn't have a tattoo, then the lover's box couldn't be what had delivered him to her house in the middle of the night. *No-o-o-o-o!* She was just about to throw herself down on the floor and wail at the unfairness of it all, when she saw that he was un-buttoning his pants.

"Uh…what are you doing?"

He grinned and her knees practically buckled. Yikes, the man had it going on. "You want to see my tattoo, right?"

Cassie nodded dumbly.

"Then I need to open my pants."

And while Cassie opened her mouth to object, somehow the words, "Give me the flashlight. You'll need your hands free," came out instead, and she didn't know which of them was more shocked.

He stilled, closed his eyes for a second, then handed her the light and went back to work on his zipper.

Well, this was certainly progressing nicely. It was all she could do not to yell out, *Thank you, Minerva.* Or wiggle the light and tell him to hurry up.

With the beam from the flashlight trained on the widening *V* of fabric at his fly as if he were a prisoner under police interrogation, she watched as dark lines of ink drawn into the writhing coils of a serpent, or maybe a dragon, arched over his hip bone. Cassie whimpered. *Yep.* It was a killer tattoo. Just as she'd written in her journal. Well, that settled that. The lover's box worked, and his ass was hers. *Yippee!*

She suddenly felt light-headed. Her mouth went dry and with each more inch that she could see of the beautiful design on his skin, the sensation grew stronger. Beneath her towel, the tiny gold key decorating her nipple became almost hot. She gasped, the tip of her breast an erotic burn. Something was happening.

His fly was halfway open, and his pants were pulled down on one side to show his hip bone. He stopped his striptease a heartbeat before he gave her the money shot and ran his finger over the portion of the tattoo he'd exposed. Cassie swallowed. The artwork looked almost alive, caressing his flesh.

He shook his head as if he was trying to clear it, then said, "This is so weird."

"You're telling me," she mumbled.

"No, I mean, it feels hot. My tattoo." At his words the tiny key at her nipple gave a responding pulse of heat.

"Oh," she gasped. She closed her eyes and swayed. She started to reach out to, well, grab him and jump his bones, but pulled the motion short. What was wrong with her? As much as she wanted to frog-march him upstairs to her bedroom and put him to work, she knew this wasn't right. Surely the man didn't just go throwing himself through glass windows whenever he felt horny.

The lover's box had done this to him and it was her fault. She was taking advantage of the poor genetically superior thing. Great, in one evening, she'd gone from desperate to sexual predator.

This didn't upset her nearly as much as she knew it should.

She cleared her throat and forced herself to take a step backward, trying to put a little distance between them. She had no flipping idea what to say. *Hello? How are you? I'm sorry that Gypsy magic brought you here tonight to satisfy my insatiable sexual demands?*

Mercifully, he spoke, sparing her the first conversational gambit. He must have noticed her step backward, because he lifted his hands and said in the sort of voice used to talk a jumper down from a ledge, "Everything's cool. I'm not going to hurt you."

Cassie figured that whimpering out, "Hurt me, baby, hurt me," would be completely inappropriate and kept her big yap shut.

Besides, the only thing she was afraid of at the moment was her bizarre *lack* of anxiety or fear. Sure, she was a bit flustered, but what female wouldn't be if faced with the sort of pulling power this guy radiated in waves. Heck, he was his own magnetic field. He'd make a dominatrix feel gauche.

What on earth had she written in her darn journal? Truthfully, she couldn't drum up an ounce of concern. She knew because she'd tried, and if this is what people meant when they talked about being comfortable with themselves and their surroundings, then this self-confidence crap was some heady stuff. Like a year's worth of therapy with a Prozac chaser.

Okay, under normal circumstances, a person would run and call 9-1-1. (That was so-o-o-o not going to happen.) Or at the very least, ask a couple of questions, like, What the hell are you doing here? At this point she didn't have much of a conscience to wrestle with in order to justify wild, pagan coupling with a complete stranger, but making sure that he knew where he was and why he was here seemed like the least she could do before she had her wicked way with him.

Cassie cleared her throat. "What's going on? I mean, is there a reason you broke my window instead of knocking on the front door?"

"YES." IT WAS THE BEST Max could manage.

He opened his mouth, still drew a blank, then closed it. Okay. This sucked. Badly. He'd finally met the lust of his life and he couldn't think of a single lame-ass excuse for why he'd broken into the place. Usually he was the high king of BS but his silver tongue was too busy imagining how great it would feel rubbing and flicking against her own to fall back into his regular brand of shinola.

Truthfully, now that he'd clapped eyes on the curvy bundle of bliss before him, he didn't give a flying flip about Rajko's box. He'd get to it later, the whole treasure thing taking a major backseat to his new reason for breathing—slipping up the siren's skimpy towel, then slipping up inside her. It was as if the second he'd seen her someone had waved the ultimate relic, like the Holy Grail or the exact GPS location of Atlantis, right under his nose.

Cocky as it sounded, Max had bedded more women than any one man should be allowed to, and he could honestly say that he'd never wanted to bump friendlies with a particular female so much in his life. *Damn.* His whole body was one massive, pounding urge. He wanted her. And he meant *wanted* her. Right now. But he needed to play it cool. Not totally scare her off before he got his hands, and a few other parts, all over her.

So far, she hadn't run screaming from the room. Definitely a mark in the positive column. He just had to figure out a way to get her onboard with the program before he died from the most rapid onset of acute blue balls in the history of mankind.

"Oh, well then…" She'd let the silence stretch interminably as she'd waited for him to continue, and clearly didn't know how to take his one-word answer. Since nothing sprang to mind that wouldn't get his face slapped, he was sticking with his brief response. She added, "That's good, I guess."

She seemed pretty mind-whacked herself, because the only thing she did was give him a look that was one part dazed, one part confused and one part I-could-eat-you-for-days-and-never-get-enough. Obviously, it was this last one that he needed to cozy up to. But how, without freaking her right the hell out…?

All right. He was not without assets. As soon as he'd been old enough to realize that boys had tallywackers and girls didn't, he'd also noticed that the poor tally-wackerless side of the species seemed to be mighty partial to the way God had made him. Had he mentioned that he was a lucky son of a bitch?

She'd also shown an unholy interest in his tattoo, which he was prepared to exploit mercilessly.

While he'd been trying to figure out a way to suavely approach her and hold her still long enough to rock their worlds, she'd gone back to staring at the heart of the dragon. And he didn't mean that as a euphemism. The dragon's chest happened to be the part of his tatt that twisted over his hip, and where her gaze seemed to have taken up permanent residence.

Excellent. He could work with this, he thought, and his libido gave him a high-five. He shifted his weight. His cargo pants cooperated and slipped to his pubic bone.

Her lashes hit her eyebrows, and she leaned closer. *That's it, sweetheart,* he said to himself, keeping a silent dialogue running. *I've got something you definitely want to see. And touch. And wrap those little rosebud lips around.*

She had to be almost a foot shorter than him, and when she bent forward, he got a clear shot right down the front of her towel. Beads of sweat popped out across his skin. Damn, she was a tiny little thing. Well, height-wise, that was. She was perfectly, fuckably proportioned everywhere else, both above and below her waist. A pocket-size Venus, with the longest stems he'd ever seen on someone so dang diminutive. He loved it. Made him feel macho as hell. All Viking marauder, and crap.

Not a vibe he'd ever gone for until he'd spotted Miss Petite Playmate, but now, it flat-out did it for him.

She licked her Cupid's-bow mouth and lifted up onto her toes as if she were trying to peer down the open fly of his pants. The dragon sent a pulse of heat that throbbed everywhere it touched his skin, absolutely erotic and some majorly freaky shit, all at the same time.

Yep, this was so weird, and he gave not a rat's ass, just plain thrilled to be here. He could barely even think about the Gypsy king's treasure and it seemed ridiculous to him that he had ever wanted anything besides this woman.

She made a startled sound and her hand flew to her right breast, her palm pressing the terry cloth to her chest. Then she mumbled, "Why does that keep happening?"

"Why does what keep happening?" he asked, then let out a hiss of air. He slid his hand to his tatt, rubbing the orgasm-inducing spike in temperature. It was a lucky coincidence that this kept her attention exactly where he wanted it. "Damn, that's hot."

She gave a little start. "You feel it, too?"

He made a hum of agreement and sidled closer, playing off her distraction. His shirt was still wrapped around his wrist, and he flung it aside. Afraid that he was a nanosecond away from going berserk and consuming her whole, he huffed out a deep breath and ran his hands through his hair.

Now his scalp stung and he still didn't have an ounce

of control. The tiny beauty followed the movement as if mesmerized. She clearly had a thing for his hair, too. *Good*. If it wouldn't have made him feel like a total dork, he'd have flipped the stuff in her face and hoped for the best.

"Oh, I'm feeling it all right. How about you?" He hardly knew what he was saying. She was only a hand-breadth away and it was killing him. He hesitated, for the first time in his life afraid of blowing what had suddenly become the most important thing in his existence. He needed her to make the first move. Or at least give him some clue, some small signal that would give him the green light.

Then she reached out and ran her fingers over the lines of his tattoo, following the jut of his hip bone. Yep, that's what he'd been waiting for. He grabbed hold of her waist, his hands damn near meeting around the delicious curve, and maneuvered her until her back hit the asinine water buffalo in the middle of the shop. His lungs were heaving and his heart was a beat away from breaking through his sternum. He stared into her huge Bambi eyes. It was too dark to be sure of their color, but they seemed to be the same deep, warm shade of honey as the pieces of hair slipping from the knot on top of her head.

"This is going to sound crazy. But I have to. I mean, you have to let me—" He broke off and shook his head. He was stuttering. He'd lost it. Big-time. "I won't do anything that you don't want me to," he tried to assure her. "But I can't wait, and—"

She reached up and grabbed two handfuls of his hair,

the flashlight that she still held clunking the side of his head, then said, "Kiss me. Please…"

Max groaned out, "Thank God," and did exactly as the lady requested. He licked deep into her mouth, chills spreading across his skin. He could have gotten off on her kiss alone. His cock felt like a living thing down the leg of his pants, straining and pushing against the fabric.

But she broke off aeons too soon, panting out, "You're sure that you're okay with this? I don't want to take advantage of you."

He frowned down at her. "I have no idea what the hell you're talking about. But I'm willing to beg, here. We on the same page?"

"Yes," she whispered. "Yes, yes, yes…" Pulling him back into the kiss, she let the flashlight drop to the floor. It hit the carpet with a muffled thump, then flicked out. Moonlight poured through the windows in the room, brighter than he remembered it being before.

With an enthusiasm that matched his own, her hands started to move, running over his shoulders and arms. Just looking at her was like hours of amazing foreplay slammed into seconds. Her touch was freakin' overkill. He leaned in to her, trying to stop his muscles from trembling, but this only made it far, far worse. Steam was going to start rising off him. He undid the clip in her hair, sending the silken mass tumbling around her shoulders.

He pressed his face to her neck. "You smell like flowers and honey. Good. So good."

Her hands slipped lower, finding his tattoo again, and

if the damn thing could have growled, it would have. Instead, *he* did, the sound an animal rumble.

"What is it? A snake?" she asked, still clearly fascinated with his ink job.

"Dragon," he answered, and she practically *oohed* in approval. "I got it years ago in Thailand—" He broke off, realizing that he'd progressed to full out babbling. And now was in *no* way the time for trivial details since he had a much better get-to-know-ya scheme in mind.

"It's beautiful," she breathed, running her palm along the design, though, from her angle, there was no way she could see it. She was probably following the warmth. He had a regular bonfire going on down there. A couple of them.

"And big…" Her voice was sluggish, blissed out.

He muttered, "It's not the only big thing down there." Corny, he admitted, but he was a guy, and he was beyond eloquent wordplay at this point. "You can look later. As much as you want. Promise."

She leaned back, making helpless little writhing movements. He had about ten seconds here, twenty tops, before he was gone. Completely. Past the point of no return. "Do you want me? Are you cool with this?" If she said no, he had no idea what he'd do. Possibly kill something. Or cry.

She let out a laugh, husky and erotic. The sound shot straight to his groin. As if that area needed more excitement. "Want you? Of course I want you. You're exactly what I asked for. You're perfect."

He started to tilt his head at the "asked for" part of

her revelation, but was quickly sidetracked by her overall meaning. He could hardly get out the jumble of words. "Good. You can have me. Every way you can think of. As long as it's soon. Very, very soon."

Her towel slipped and she bit her lip. Her right breast popped free and moonlight glittered from the little ring at her nipple. Something dangled from the bottom curve of the hoop, and she covered it with her fingers as if to relieve an ache.

An extra heartbeat started pounding in his cock, his entire length swelling beyond any previous limits. Her nipple ring was the sexiest thing he'd ever seen.

She moaned. "Warm…so warm. I'm on fire."

His voice hoarse, he said, "You're not the only one." Puff, the now-magical dragon, sent an answering wash of flame along his hip. Oh, yeah, this was so flipping weird. And he loved it. Abso-fucking-lutely loved it.

He lowered her arm, then lowered his lips. "Here, let me help you." He gave a gentle swipe of his tongue, tasting her nipple and the tiny piece of jewelry. It was like licking melted sugar. He sucked the hoop between his teeth, tugging softly. The ring and the little charm were surprisingly hot, erotically searing the inside of his mouth and setting his blood to a rapid boil.

She arched into him. "More…. Do it more…."

He sucked harder, flicking his tongue back and forth across the ring, playing and worrying it, following her gasps and chasing every cry of pleasure groaning from her throat.

Meanwhile, she was busily working her own agenda.

Her splayed hands had staked an unholy claim on his stomach, seemingly content to hang out indefinitely and drive him right from his skin. She rubbed the bands of muscles, appearing particularly thrilled with the diagonal obliques that pointed toward his groin. Up and down, over and back, she stroked and caressed until his eyes all but rolled back in his head. As she played there for the foreseeable future, causing the tissue beneath his skin to contract and jerk, he gave the towel a small pull and it dropped to her waist.

He let her nipple slip from his mouth with a soft *thwip*. He looked down at her breasts. The moon's unusually bright glow spilled over the high, firm globes. Ridiculously lush and plump, they were almost too big for her frame, her rib cage small in comparison. His hands trembled and he somehow managed to choke out a curse. "I swear you have the most beautiful tits I've ever seen. I could look at them forever and never get tired."

Max winced, unable to believe he'd said that out loud. He'd sounded about sixteen, except more crass. But he wasn't going to lie. Her body plain floored him, in the best possible way.

She stilled, though her breath started soughing a mile a minute. "Do you really mean that?"

He gave a rueful laugh. "Uh, yeah. Every word." Lord, he was such an ass.

Though, bizarrely, she appeared to be more thrilled than if he'd spouted the most romantic of love poems. *Damn*. She just kept getting more and more perfect. But why? Why would such a beautiful, beyond sexy woman act surprised? She had to have heard the sentiment from every man who'd ever been lucky enough to see her.

However, he wasn't exactly in the frame of mind to ponder mysteries and was immediately distracted by the most effective diversionary tactic he'd ever witnessed. She cupped her breasts and lifted them in her palms. They didn't need the support, since the plump pair were a gravity-defying miracle all on their own, but this was the equivalent of offering them up to him on a platter. Permission and invitation to take his pleasure from her body.

"Don't you still want me?"

A low buzz started in his muscles, vibrating down to the bone. His nostrils flared. "Uh-huh. But in one more second I won't be able to stop. I've never wanted a woman so much. It's like I have to have you and if I don't…" he shook his head "—well, that would be bad…really, really bad…."

This time, after he spoke, she all but beamed up at him. It was unfathomable to him that she had doubts about her desirability since mere moments in her presence had him acting completely out of character. Max was a seducer, not a taker. And if she didn't let him take her soon, he had no doubt that he would add beggar and pleader to his new set of skills.

It certainly wasn't the voice of a slick player that rasped, "So, um, we're cool, right? I mean, we're feeling the same vibe?"

He took her whimper as a yes, and had to clamp his jaw closed to keep from making the sound along with her. He slid his palms beneath her breasts. Unable to help himself, he gave them a little bounce, testing their weight, and that's all it took. He groaned and slammed his mouth down against hers. That quickly they were back up at full speed, both of them frantic, breath whooshing through their nostrils, and bodies shaking and bucking against the other's.

While he tweaked and rubbed her nipples her own hands got down to business and there was no more screwing around. She pushed his pants to the middle of his thighs, and wrapped her greedy fingers around his swollen shaft as it bobbed free. His knees almost buckled and he locked them in place, shifting his feet apart to widen his stance. Sensation sizzled down the length of his arousal and he had to fight not to dance away from her touch, or to do the exact opposite and thrust and shove himself into her hand. Okay, that was enough prep time for him.

But with the differences in their heights, this was not going to work unless he propped her up somewhere, and while he'd use it if he had to, he preferred not to do the nasty with her up against the frigging water buffalo. Frantically, he looked around the room, trying to make out the various shapes and shadows. He spotted one of those huge ottomans that could double as a coffee table. He lifted her up and swung her around, her towel fluttering to the floor. Dropping her sweet bottom onto the velvet, Max hit his knees in front of her. It aligned them perfectly, and he slipped his elbow beneath her knee and spread her wide, resting his hand next to her hip for leverage.

She grabbed onto his hair again, pulling his mouth down to hers, and their tongues rubbed and slid against each other like long-lost friends.

His entire body felt like a massive exposed nerve as he skimmed his other hand down through the delicate lace of curls at the top of her mound. His middle finger shook as he slipped it between her hot, wet labia. She was drenched, cream soaking his skin, and she cried out. As wet as she was, he had to work first one, then two, fingers up inside her, holding her open with his arm beneath her leg. "You're tight as a fist," he ground out.

She moaned, then squeezed his ass, which thrust him against her core. His poor cock hardly withstood the sensory overload, her actions causing the underside of his shaft to rub against his own forearm and palm, which were already busy down there, pleasuring her. The head caressed her petal-soft lips, slid on her thick dew up to brush through her feathery curls.

All right, that was it. He wanted in. Now.

He somehow gasped through his busy mouth, "Your hands are closer. Grab my wallet. Back pocket." To reach, she had to sit up straighter, arching her spine. Her nipples seared his pecs, the little ring catching and tugging against his chest hair with each jerky movement.

"Got it," she mumbled around his tongue.

He broke their kiss, his lungs heaving, and said, "Flip it open. Condoms are in the slot."

She pulled out a string of them, about four or five, then held them up and laughed. "Woo-hoo. I guess the box not only covered all the bases, but was pretty optimistic that we'd have more than one go."

As for the number of condoms in his wallet, well… the less said the better. Though he wasn't about to tell her that. Also, he had no idea what she meant.

"I just threw what I had in there. Now I'm hoping they'll be enough." So far everything he'd admitted was absolutely true, but with the added bonus of his not sounding like some sleazebag always on the prowl. He usually didn't need to bother with the prowling. Again, the less said the better, and it was all completely irrelevant anyway since she was definitely in a class by herself, and he'd have crawled over broken glass to get to her.

"You. Are. Perfect," she said, her voice both amused and awed.

Trying to joke back, he said, "I'll show you perfect. Either hand me one, or get busy." But he was way too far over the edge for kidding around. He closed his eyes, and clenched his jaw as she rolled the lubed rubber down his length. When she finished, she fondled his sack, giving firm squeezes that sent jolts up and down his spine. Pressure grew in his lower back and he could feel his balls pull in tight.

Taking his fingers out of her slick center, he gently moved her hand away in case she ended the whole show before they even got to the good part, then used his thumb to push down on his shaft. The fat head slipped between her inner lips, and she started panting in earnest. Slowly, he pressed his way into her burning core. His body trembled. *Yep*. She was tiny, all right. *Everywhere…*

She gulped, then he heard her mumbling under her breath, something about going overboard and how she should have been more specific with the whole *thick* and *large* part of her list.

She hardly made sense whenever she spoke, but she was a goddess, so he mostly overlooked her confusing chatter.

Max didn't want to hurt her and the angle was too sharp with her sitting straight up. He rubbed her hip, then moved his hand to the center of her back and slowly lowered her until she was lying on the ottoman.

There had to be the fullest of moons out tonight— the werewolves howling, crazy people going wonkers kind of full—because the pale glow pouring through the windows bathed her like a lunar spotlight. It was surreal, every detail like a fantasy come to life.

He gazed down at her spread out before him. His breath froze in his lungs. A low hum vibrated through his frame, and if he hadn't been one-hundred-percent desperate, he could've stared forever.

"Don't stop…" she urged, rocking her pelvis so that she slid and squeezed the thick tip of his cock firmly lodged inside her tight heat with each restless little circle. One of her legs was still hitched on his elbow, and he shifted the other into matching position, spreading her wide and leaning forward, using his weight to push deeper.

Pleasure punched him in the gut. He grit his teeth. He had to go slow, her inner walls were too narrow to force his way without hurting her. But, so far, just being halfway in was better than anything he'd ever felt. Keeping her legs hooked over his arms, he moved his hands to her waist, his grip firm as he pulled her backside to the very edge of the ottoman. The leverage all his, he slowly dragged back his hips, then let the weight of his lower body sink into her again.

His chest hovered above hers, caging her in and pressing her legs up and out. The porn-star pose was impossibly arousing, too erotic to watch, and he had to look away or he'd come. She moaned and squirmed, then slid her fingers back into his hair, her favorite spot when she wasn't petting and torturing his abs. Her sweet mouth sucked onto his, her tongue delving deep, wreaking havoc with each sensual swirl.

Rocking and pushing, he finally worked in all of his thick length to the hilt and they both gasped. Then his eyes widened, and a raw sound broke from his throat.

"Don't move. Oh, God, do…not…move…." Muscles flexed with tension, he forced himself to hold perfectly still. Now, Max had his flaws just like the next guy, but premature ejaculation had sure as hell never been one them. Ever. Period. End of discussion and draw a line under it. So why the hell did he feel like a frigging virgin would have a better chance at lasting longer in the hot seat?

Mindlessly, she shook her head back and forth, definitely craving the same thing he was, though probably not the two-pump version that was looking more and more likely. His hands clamped down on the top of her thighs, fingers biting into her skin, stopping her mind-numbing undulations.

She bit her lip, and moaned, "But I want to move…."

His voice lower than he'd ever heard, he somehow managed to say, "I won't last. Sorry. Crap," he broke off and squeezed his eyes shut. "I don't know what's wrong." He tried to slow his breathing, but his lungs were blasting out air. "I had to get inside you. More than anything. But it's too good." He shook his head. "Way…too…good…"

If she'd seemed strangely pleased by his other juvenile comments, then she appeared downright thrilled at his latest embarrassing disclosure.

She shoved her pelvis up against his, sending a shower of sparks flashing behind his retinas, and said, "Yes. It's exactly how I fantasized…. Do it. Hurry…." Then she clapped her hands down on his ass, and his eyes shot wide as she pulled him impossibly deep. "Now," she gasped, "please. Now…."

He started to be shocked then decided he plain didn't care, began plunging into her, and hung on for dear life. She bucked and writhed while his body took over. Pressure swelled through his lower stomach and up the backs of his thighs. He lunged, his buttocks flexing as he worked his length in and out, stronger and harder. His tattoo had become the hot depths of the earth, radiating pulses of ecstasy, his skin one massive erogenous zone. His heartbeat pounded in his ears and his hips started to lose their rhythm.

Her breasts wobbled beneath him, bounced in tempo with each frantic thrust, making her cry out and sob, clearly loving every damn minute of it. Her nipple ring was its own little circle of fire, and he wouldn't be completely surprised if it left a brand on his chest by the time this whole thing was finished. Speaking of finished…

"Come on, come on," he softly urged, his lips against the delicate shell of her ear. He needed her to come before he did, this gorgeous, sexy gift. He wanted to worship her, bring her over and over, but the most he'd managed was to bang the living daylights out of her.

Then he found her mouth, caught it with his own, and poured every ounce of concentration into the stroke and glide of his tongue and his erection. Within seconds she convulsed under him so hard that her hips actually lifted up his lower body for the first few brutal beats of her orgasm.

Her slick heat squeezed and milked his length in vise-tight spasms, and Max gave himself up. The pressure in his gut blew wide. A tidal wave of release slammed into him, and the damn thing didn't stop, spurting and jetting with exquisite agony beyond anything he'd ever experienced. His body jerked and shuddered. Then, after several long moments, it was done, and eternal minutes later, he survived the aftermath with only the occasional twitch and shiver.

He slumped to the side, because the last thing he wanted to do was crush his brand-new best friend. Finally finding his voice, he cleared his throat past the gravel, and started to ask, "You okay?" but was cut off by the jingle of shattering glass from another room.

She went stiff in his hold as they heard, somewhere

in a back room of the store, the very obvious sound of a window being forced and shoved open.

Minerva really needed to have the windows in this place fixed, Max thought absently. Made breaking in hell. Practically as noisy as kicking in the damn front door. Then he cursed when he realized that another bastard was doing exactly what he'd been doing before he'd gotten sidetracked by the premier sexual encounter of his life.

"No way.... This can't be happening," she whispered.

Looking over his shoulder in the direction he'd heard the din coming from, he reached down to yank up his pants, and started to push himself upright. He couldn't help but be stopped short, though, by more of her confusing babble, and he jerked his head toward her. "Huh?"

"I can't believe this," she said softly. "I did *not* ask for two of you...."

4

No freakin' way.... Cassie scowled, her thoughts scrambling. As if earlier tonight, back in her bedroom, she'd written down some fantasy for a threesome. Two guys and her. *Puh-lease.*

Though, on a side note, she had no idea how much Minerva had paid for the lover's box, but talk about getting maximum bang for your buck. Her fantasy had come true and then some.

"Hurry. Come on," her dream lover urged, trying to sit her up and wrap her back in the towel, which he must have retrieved from somewhere by the water buffalo's feet. She was never going to be able to look at that beast in the same way, and suddenly felt quite fondly toward the stuffed eyesore.

"Is there another way out of here?" he asked, breaking into her pleasant post-nooky haze.

Since he was still whispering, she whispered back, "What do you mean?"

He'd started to turn away from her, then did a double take. "What do you mean, what do I mean? Someone's breaking into the house." He was much better at the whispering thing than her. His low voice was barely audible, but she could still make out every word.

Not a big giggler, Cassie, nonetheless, found herself making the ridiculous sound. "Well, the last time that happened, it worked out pretty well for me."

"You're crazy, you know that? Nothing you say makes sense."

She smiled, in too good a mood to fight. Amazing sex will do that to a gal. He merely cursed, then shook his head.

"Whoever's back there better not get the same welcome I just did. Hear me? You're mine." As if surprised by what he'd said, he stopped, then frowned even more.

He shook his head again, muttering under his breath, "Stay here." He crouched down, and as luminous as the glow from outside was, the second he moved away he blended into the shadows.

His he-man "stay here" order didn't bother her. With après-Gypsy-lovin' languor stealing through her limbs, she'd rather avoid any action that didn't directly involve his naked body.

Before she knew it, though, her fantasy lover was back, giving off a whole new kind of tension. He grabbed her upper arms, jerking her to her feet, and she gasped. She caught the towel to her chest while his hand covered her mouth, not hard, but the message obvious: do not make a sound. He said directly into her ear, "There are three of them. I know who they are."

Cassie's eyes flew wide. Her eyebrows stretched

toward her hairline and she held up three fingers toward his face. He nodded distractedly, craning his neck around while scanning the room. *Three?!* That would give her a total of four men. What the hell sort of fantasies did that freaky lover's box think she was into?

Then she hesitated, flashing a quick grin behind his palm, and thought, *Then again, if they take after Mega-Handsome the Sex Stud here, maybe I could put them on a rotating schedule. Draw up a roster, or something.* Had her social life done a one-eighty or what?

His gaze trained on the hallway that led to the back storage room, he started directing her toward the window that he'd broken through.

"Gla-a-ath-h-h," she mumbled against the inside of his hand.

"What?"

She grabbed his wrist and pulled it away. "Glass," she hissed softly, nodding toward the shards on the floor. "I'll cut my feet."

He stopped and immediately pulled her into his chest as if he hadn't been the one pushing her forward. "Sorry," he breathed, looking down. "You need shoes."

"You need to stop worrying," she answered, still using her we'll-be-in-deep-petooty-if-someone-hears-us voice. It kept a level of intimacy between them that she was wa-a-a-ay into. "Look, I'll just tell these guys, whoever they are, that I don't need them. That you're more than up to handling the job solo, but thanks anyway." She couldn't help it, and ran her fingers over his stomach, bumping up and down his rock-hard muscles.

He closed his eyes and put his hand over hers, trapping it. "You're so sexy, you make my teeth ache, but I don't get a thing you say. Not one word. It might as well be Swahili. Although *that,* I can speak."

She cocked her head, "You speak Swahili? Cool."

He sucked in a breath, his nostrils flaring. "Not important." It was amazing the amount of censor he could convey while keeping his voice only a decibel above a dog's hearing. "Those guys in there might not be killers, but they're ruthless. I need to get you out of here and get the bo—"

She interrupted, "I hate to break the news to you, gorgeous, but you ain't exactly crystal clear, yourself. What on earth are you talking about?"

"What am *I* talking about? I—" He bit off whatever else he was going to say and closed his eyes. "This is like being stuck in a frigging Abbott and Costello movie." He'd have kept on scolding her, no doubt, but a floorboard creaked in the back hallway. Immediately, he clapped his hand over her mouth again. Then, in one move, he turned her and smashed her back to his front, gluing them together.

He wrapped his arm around her waist like a steel band and, after a fast glance around the room, picked her up, then moved them behind a fake sarcophagus looming nearby. In the waiting silence, she was suddenly aware that the man jammed up close and personal to the entire back half of her body had turned menacingly still as he tracked the movements of the latest fellas whom the lover's box had sent.

It was as if a dead calm had come over him, and he'd become dangerous. She didn't question how she knew, she just did. It was the same instinct one had when facing a predator. The weaker animal didn't analyze the wheres and whys, it merely got the heck out of Dodge. For the first time, she felt a tingle of alarm creep up her spine. Though her instincts also told her that his lethal aura was not directed against her but at the new arrivals.

His full, beautiful mouth returned to her ear, and he breathed, "These men will hurt you if you don't give them what they want. This isn't a game. I can take them on, but I can't protect you while I'm beating the hell out of them. Quickest exit. Just move your chin as if you're pointing to it."

Okay. Now he was scaring her. Sort of. Strangely, it was more like an adrenaline rush than the true scaredy-cat stuff she usually felt. Why didn't he believe they could take out these guys? Granted, she wouldn't be doing much of the taking-out portion, but she could certainly keep from harm's way. She was not the dopey sort of heroine that she saw in movies who cried and made a big mess of everything, then got the hero caught and herself taken hostage.

Wait a second. Her eyes widened and she jerked her chin toward the foyer at the north side of the store, past the arched entryway customers used. If they went in that direction, they could go out the front door or go straight through to the private section of the house and up the staircase that led to the top floor.

What had she been thinking? Normally, she was

exactly that sort of stupid female she saw in movies, except without the crying. An expert at making big messes and generally screwing things up, she usually saved the tears for her own private pity party. For some reason, though, at the moment, she was feeling more Linda Hamilton à la *Terminator 2* than Lucille Ball à la the "Candy Factory" episode.

Huh. The kick-ass part of her fantasy must have started. She wondered if this was only a false confidence or if she'd somehow mystically gained tough-girl skills, too. But she wasn't given the opportunity to find out.

He must've understood the chin nod, because his arm tightened around her waist again and they were mobile. Moving from shadow to shadow, her body tucked in front of his, they made it to the foyer without being spied. With the size of the store's main room and all the ridiculous junk Minerva had crammed in the place, this wasn't quite as difficult as one might assume. And, as in most older homes, with the vestibule its own separate area, no one could see them now that they'd gained their current position.

After their serpentine trek, however, Cassie's wits had returned and she realized that his behavior was even more delusional than she'd thought since there wasn't a chance in hell that three men would hurt her to "get what they came for." Gypsy magic or no, she was a far cry from femme fatale or Playmate of the month. Obviously, she must have left some loophole for more than one lover when she'd written in her diary. Still, she seriously doubted they'd resort to fisticuffs when she refused to do them.

Cassie sighed, and shook her head as if she could wipe her thoughts clean. This whole fiasco was getting more and more ludicrous. She actually possessed the ability to procure unlimited fantasy sex, and, as per her usual outstanding luck, everything was going screwy and men were pouring in the windows.

Yes, yes, it sounded like the ultimate problem to have, but not with double-*O*-handsome acting as if danger lurked at every corner and believing there were bad guys out to get them. Besides, she didn't think that they were in any real peril, only Gypsy-magic peril. But how could she explain that to Prince Sexy without sounding like a total crackpot?

His body right next to hers, he lowered his head and spoke in that eerie hushed voice of his. "We use this door, they'll hear and come after us. Can we get to the back of the house without going through the shop?"

Cassie opened her mouth to argue, then shrugged and shut up. Bringing him to a side passage in the recesses of the foyer, she moved the Staff Only sign that roped it off, and led him into the house's original dining room, then onward into the kitchen. She might as well get him someplace where she could speak her peace without his clamping his hand over her mouth every two seconds.

She put her foot on the bottom stair, ready to continue on up to her room so she could get dressed or screw his brains out again once this pesky multiple partner crap had been cleared up—honestly, she didn't care who else the lover's box had sent. She'd hit pay dirt here and was sticking with the hunk she knew rather than the three she didn't. But, he stopped her with a hand gripped to the back of her towel.

Speaking fast, he whispered, "No. You need to leave before Victor's goons realize you're here."

She didn't know who Victor was, nor give a rip about him or his goons. Though all she said was, "In a towel," her voice dry.

He hesitated. "It's better than some of the other possibilities. Look, I don't have time to argue. Your aunt sent you a package. Did you get it?"

A big red flag popped up in Cassie's brain and started flapping like mad. She licked her lips. How did he know about the lover's box? And how did he know that Minerva had sent it?

Although, she supposed that seeing as the box was a conduit for mind-numbing fantasy sex, it should not come as a complete surprise that he would have knowledge of its existence and her recent ownership.

Cassie sighed and waved her hand. "Yes," she answered.

"Yes, you got the package, and yes, you have it?"

They had to stop doing this. Even she was getting a bit tetchy at their convoluted conversations. And she got to look at him while they spoke. He must be ready to shove a blunt object in his ear.

"Yes," she said, her impatience obvious. "Yes to both."

"Good. Tell me where it is, then wait for me outside." He stepped in close, totally distracting her.

Almost immediately, though, he stiffened as if he'd made a mistake, because, in a snap, his entire presence turned from dangerous to erotic. Cassie stared at him, stupefied.

Then some of the wording that she'd written into her fantasy floated through her mind—*a man so filled with lust that whenever he saw her, all he could think about was getting inside her.* Check. *A single glance and he was stone hard.* Cassie took a quick peek at his crotch and gulped. Check. *Bullets could be whizzing over their heads and he'd want her.* Oh, lordy, there wasn't any artillery fire, but still… She turned her gaze to his face and his expression was magnificently filled with sexual intent. She gulped again. Check.

But before she could figure out how to clear up the snafu, he said, "We don't have time for this." He dropped his hand to her bottom, then rubbed and stroked as if he were driven by an overwhelming surge of primitive desire. His voice was a sensual rumble that she swore made things vibrate inside her. "I can't stop…. I know I should, but…"

She practically purred when he caressed his fingertips over her lower cheeks then slowly ran them up and down the crack that separated the curvy globes. Up and down. Up and down. And, yes, *curvy* was the kindest description she'd allow herself. *Hello.* She was only five foot two. Too much junk in the trunk was pretty much a standard problem.

Then the full reality of his devastating touch hit her, and Cassie thought, *Oh…my…gosh….* She rose up on her toes, and squirmed against his hand.

"You're coming with me," he said, and from the bottom of her heart, she hoped that his word choice had not been accidental. "Now that Victor's men know about you, and have tracked me to the shop, you won't be safe here. At least for a day or two. Or three. Possibly a week. We'll go to a hotel. Me and you and a bed. As long as I've got the box, the treasure can wait." He closed his eyes, as if he were fighting himself and losing.

"We need to leave now. Right now. Well…just as soon as I do this, and—" He broke off his words to slide his two fingertips up to the top of her crease then down to rub the stretch of skin right behind her dampening sheath.

His other hand went beneath her hair to the back of her neck, his palm warm and steady as she shivered. He was stiff everywhere. And she meant *everywhere*.

Now that Cassie thought about it, she didn't believe that she'd given herself enough time earlier to rhapsodize and praise the virtues of his amazing erection. She promptly focused on the object of her desire and it was all she could do not to swoon like a Southern belle.

Instead, she touched his lower stomach then slid her fingers over the tough fabric and down to his brutal length, which punched against the fly of his pants. Nothing should feel this good, and she couldn't stop her quiet groan of bliss.

His voice a husky rasp, his mouth moved against hers as he said, "Let's get my box and get out of here." But she wasn't really paying attention to his words. His smoocher was a work of art. His top lip was perfectly chiseled and the bottom begged to be bitten. Full and almost pouty, both of them together formed a wide, irresistible curve. Modeling agencies would commit acts of war to get him in their ads.

"I'll take care of Victor and his thugs later," he went on. "I won't let them hurt you. Ever. I promise."

Her eyebrows drew together, but when she went to speak, his thumb on the back of her neck moved in soothing circles while his other glided ever downward then, from behind, dipped inside her wet heat, rotating.

Her head would have fallen back if not for his hand. She somehow managed to say, "You mean *my* box…." Though why, if he truly thought they were in danger, was he so concerned with getting the lover's box before he left? Sure, fantasy sex might be high on *her* list, but this guy had to be living it every time he felt the urge.

Cassie ground down on his thumb and the base of his palm, needing him deeper. He hesitated, then said, "I'm a relic hunter like Minerva." He stopped to kiss her, one hot, slick swipe of his tongue. "I bought the lover's box in St. Petersburg. She stole it. But she's not getting the treasure," he grated out, showing that physically he was faring little better than her.

She frowned and whispered, "You know Minerva?"

His nod was distracted, his thumb making a swivel as he slowly pumped it in then out, over and over. His whisper deep and raspy, he answered, "Yeah, I know her. The box is mine. And when I find it, so is the treasure."

With the sensual fog enveloping her brain, she could barely focus on his words. Within moments, though, enough of the important ones got through. She stiffened, then squirmed and wiggled out of his hold. He took one last shocking liberty among all her slippery wetness before he let her go, and she almost cried out, *oh, to hell with it,* and wiggled back into place.

But all she did was blink and ask dumbly, "You think the lover's box is yours?"

He grunted. "I don't think it. I know it."

"I can't believe this," she snapped.

"Shh" he said, looking back toward the kitchen.

She pointed to her chest and tapped it. "The box is mine. You're here because—" She stopped, not anxious to admit that Gypsy magic had brought him here in the middle of the night to service her insatiable sexual demands. But, come on, as if she was supposed to believe some stupid story about his being a thrill-seeking relic hunter like her great-aunt, and that the lover's box was really his, and they'd merely hooked up as an aside when he'd shown up to steal it back.

Cassie stilled. Oh, crap.

She asked herself what made more sense—that an almost century-old Gypsy spell had made her fantasy come true, or that the wily Minerva was up to one of her crazy antics and had stolen the lover's box from this man.

A wash of heat crept up Cassie's face, hotter than the silly nipple ring that all night had kept pulsing on and off like a demented firefly. And how did she explain *that* strange aspect of this fiasco? It didn't matter. Probably hormones, or something equally mundane. Like her nipple having an allergic reaction to metal.

Why did she keep doing things like this? Foolishly holding out hope that the ridiculous and unimaginable was true. Oh, like, say, believing her ex-fiancé had really loved her and just had a low sex drive, rather than accepting that he was an amoral cheat who'd married another woman within two weeks of breaking up with her. Su-u-ure he'd met the *real* love of his life the day he'd moved out of their apartment. Ri-i-ight....

Hell. She was a total moron. No wonder she'd believed in the stupid legend of the lover's box. Apparently, a deep-seated core of gullibility plagued her psyche. Talk about a bummer.

Cassie took a step away from him, rubbing her forehead while creeping up the next rise of the staircase. It was all too confusing and humiliating. Could nothing in her life be simple? Other than her brain.

She knew he could have stopped her if he wanted to, but he allowed her to back away. She didn't bother thanking him, assuming that putting out for the guy within five minutes of clapping eyes on him was thanks enough.

She supposed she really shouldn't be so upset that Gypsy magic hadn't brought him to her, but she was. Because if the lover's box wasn't fueling their encounter, then she wasn't recklessly living out a fantasy. At best, she was no better than the probably hundreds of other women who'd turned insta-slut the second they'd caught a glimpse of the gorgeous freak. At worst, it left him seducing her merely so that she would be more amenable when he stole the lover's box from her. Or maybe he'd just assumed that she'd hand it over to him as a sign of her deep and profound thanks for generously gifting her with the use of his body. Not a bad assumption on his part, she had to admit.

In spite of the zenith of orgasms that the jerk had brought her to and all, this majorly sucked.

Cassie turned and started marching up the stairs. "Do not even think it," she practically snarled when he reached out to stop her.

Right then she heard a noise from the store. The three stooges, whomever they were, were most likely ransacking the place. Okay. So she should have called 9-1-1 when she'd spotted her first home invader. *Go figure.*

"Where's the box?" he grated as he kept pace two steps below her. This probably put her huge butt right smack-dab at face level. Fitting punishment, in her opinion.

"Who the hell are you?" she shot over her shoulder.

He was quiet for a moment, then rasped, "You have the sweetest ass...."

Cassie rolled her eyes. Right. "Yeah, well, you can go ahead and kiss it while you're back there," she said as snarkily as possible. Then added, "whoever you are," at the same time he said, "Can I really?" sounding inordinately hopeful.

She really wished that he'd go ahead and drop the whole seduction routine. Now that she realized Gypsy voodoo wasn't fueling the attraction from his side, she knew there was no way this fiendishly beautiful creep would ever give her a second glance, let alone be desperate to possess her.

She hadn't even been able to keep a dull-o creep like Ron on the line. Never mind snag the interest of an adrenaline junky like this fella. Relic hunters were thrill seekers addicted to the excitement of the chase. Minerva and her cronies were all the same. A person only took up hunting antiquities or other treasures because they loved adventure. The idea of his being filled with lust after a single glance at *her* was a total joke.

Cassie pulled her mouth into a sneer. From Ron to this. She was cursed.

She reached the landing and was about to storm into her bedroom, door banging against the wall, all dramatic entry and junk, when she paused. If her fantasy hadn't brought lover boy here tonight, then it hadn't been responsible for the arrival of the men downstairs, either.

She flattened her lips, then rolled them inward and took a deep breath through her nose. All right. Bad guys were really after her and she might want to hold off on reaming this fella a new one until she was in a safe environment. Like calling him from her cell phone when she got to the police station.

Back to tiptoeing so as not to make noise, she made her way into her room. She didn't bother with the lights since she knew he'd have a cow if she so much as raised her hand toward the switch.

The handsome shadow from hell whispered behind

her, "I don't know what you're so pissed off about. I'm the one who was robbed by your crazy aunt. I only came here to get my damn box back."

If he couldn't figure out that this was a huge part of the problem, then she wasn't about to set him straight. In fact, hearing him fess up to his motives merely ticked her off more. "Yeah, well, the forecast is predicting I'll get even bitchier. Deal with it."

He sounded like he was gritting his teeth. "Listen. Just get the lover's box so we can get out of here."

"The lover's box is mine. Possession is nine-tenths of the law." Cassie had no idea if this was really true or not, but people were always throwing the line around in legal shows. "And *we're* not going anywhere," she whispered furiously. As if she was going to hang around with this paragon of manly prowess.

"What the hell is your name, anyway?"

He hesitated, shifting his weight, his entire demeanor suddenly seeming embarrassed. "Max Stone. I know you're Minerva's great-niece, but your name is…?"

"Cassie Parker," she grumbled, never before having experienced the special joy of introducing herself to a man after she'd already done the naked boogie with him.

His teeth flashed bright against his face (would the moon *please* slip behind a cloud for cripes sake, so she could stop getting such a good look at him), and he said, "Well, Cassie, it's been a pleasure to meet you."

Cassie snorted. "It was all mine, I'm sure." So she could be a major witch. She felt justified after having her pagan hopes of fulfilling her sexual desires till dying of old age dashed upon the rocky shoals of disappointment. Also, the thought of never again fooling around with Max Stone was enough to make her infinitely pissy.

He sighed. "I feel like I ask this question about every fifth time I speak, but what are you talking about?"

She really didn't feel like doing this right now, especially if they were supposed to be working toward a quick getaway. But, then again, she was a fully functioning female and arguing over guy-girl stuff always took precedence over life-and-death situations, and she answered, "It's obvious you just seduced me to get to the lover's box. Ew."

He actually laughed, then cut off the sound when he apparently realized this didn't jibe with being the master of all that was stealth.

Her not-so-fantasy lover loomed over her, as he was wont to do. Then, his voice an erotic tease, he said, "Damn. You figured me out. Downstairs, when you saw me come through the window..." He shook his head. "I knew right off that there was no way I could take on a Goliath like you. Sex was my only hope at that point. A sacrifice, but I survived."

Cassie narrowed her eyes. "Hey. No short jokes."

While he snickered, she stalked to her closet and grabbed her backpack, then started throwing things inside. Fine. She'd go with him for now. Better the sexy asshole she knew, than the dangerous three she didn't.

Since time was probably of the essence, she picked up the pace, rushing into her bathroom and snagging only the essentials: toothbrush, most of her makeup and her birth control pills. Hey, just because she hated him didn't mean she had to go around looking like a washed-out hag. And if she skipped her pills, she'd jump-start her period. Not fun.

Cassie hurried back and noticed the lover's box on her bedside table. She snatched it up and pushed it into her backpack.

"You just left it sitting out in the open?" he whispered.

"How was I to know my house was going to turn into Thieves-Gone-Wild?" She snorted, quickly looking around her room to make sure she wasn't forgetting anything. "My great-aunt gave it to me as a present. It would have been unmannerly to stick it in a bottom drawer."

Oops. Clothes might be nice. Keeping the backpack at her feet, she dropped her towel, then hurriedly pulled on the first things her hands touched when they reached into her closet. Let him look all he wanted. She was so mad at him, he deserved to see her naked—in all her underwhelming glory. Remind him of how low he'd sunk just to get a crappy antique.

He growled. There was no other description for the noise he made as she bent over to wiggle into her jeans. She was slipping her feet into her sneakers and reaching for a top when he said, "I'm riding the edge here, short-stuff. Don't push me."

Cassie stiffened. *Shortstuff?!* Now he'd gone too far. She turned to blast him, and her nose skidded through his light dusting of chest hair. *Dang it*. How did he sneak around so quietly? He *was* the master of all that was stealth.

His enticing scent filled her nostrils, shoved up against him as she was, and she breathed deeply until her lungs practically popped. It was all she could do not to purr and nuzzle in for a nice long visit. She wasn't even going to address the gleeful reactions her bare breasts were experiencing. The girls had gone to a much better place…and she hated to drag them away.

His big body actually trembled and he jerked the shirt from her hand, unfolded it with a snap of his wrist, then tugged it down her torso.

Scowling, she shoved her arms through the stretchy sleeves. She brushed her hair out of her face. "I didn't get to put on a bra," she groused.

He gripped her upper arms, his fingers kneading convulsively. "Leave it. You didn't put on any panties, either," he rasped, acting as if just talking about her underwear was doing it for him. "We don't have time."

"You can quit your I-must-have-you-now act. I'm going with you." Yes, she was dumb, but not dumb enough to stick around this hotbed of larcenous activity.

His fingers tightened on her arms to just this side of *ow, ow, ow*. He finally lost his low-level whisper to complain, "You think this is an act?" Then he pumped his value-size arousal against her stomach and groaned like a dying man.

And right then and there Cassie decided that she might have been a tad hasty in her angry reaction to his seduction routine for the lover's box. If this is how he wanted to play it, then more power to him and maybe they could have one for the road. A quickie before they made their escape.

Before she could make her offer, however, her bedroom door crashed open behind them. Her three other burglars had dropped by for their playdate. *Oh, goody.*

Max immediately shoved her behind him, going straight into crouching-hottie-hidden-dragon mode, his fists flying. He took on the men like a freakin' gladiator. She had no more than a moment to even register the spectacle when, from the corner of her eye, she saw a dark shadow lunge directly for her. Without thought, she threw herself backward onto her bed and somersaulted, legs flipping into the air. On the way over, her foot caught the baddie's chin, his head slamming back with a startled *oof,* while she finished the maneuver and came up standing on the other side.

Cassie gaped. She'd never moved like that before in her life, her actions pure reflex. Max did a double take, then barked at her to run like hell. And if he'd been fighting dirty before, he went downright insane now that one of the goons had made a grab for her.

Meanwhile, she was trying to figure out how she'd managed to pull that off. But she didn't have time to come up with an answer.

She heard a rush of air and automatically ducked. The body of another goon crashed into the bedside table next to her. The lamp that had been resting on it fell into her hands like a gift and, quick as a flash, she brought it down on the back of the guy's skull. He moaned, then slumped to the carpet, no longer moving.

She turned back to the fight and watched Max finish off the third goon with a brutal right hook. Damn. Then her fantasy lover clamped his hand down on her wrist and ran.

5

"I LIKE YOUR WHEELS. Nice get-away truck," Cassie said between gasps, trying to sound as withering as possible with her lungs screaming for oxygen. "Is it just me, though, or could you not have parked any farther away from my house?"

Max shot her a look. "We're only a couple of blocks away." He slammed the door, rocking the beat-up truck. She knew he wasn't particularly angry at her comment, merely in a hurry. Also, he probably needed the momentum just to get the dented thing to swing shut.

She clutched the backpack in her lap, looking back and forth between the windshield and rear window to keep an eye out for nebulous bad guys giving chase. After Max had won enough rounds of the WWE *Smack-Down* back in her bedroom, he'd all but dragged her in his swift, athletic wake.

She hadn't complained, though. As they'd scrambled out of the house she'd imagined some tough muscle car waiting nearby—him sliding across the hood, her jumping into the passenger seat, and then she and Max speeding away in a blaze of badass glory.

One street over, and a slew of her neighbors' yards a memory beneath her feet, she'd wheezed for him to get the car and come back for her. He'd ignored her and run faster. Could she help it if her hobbies were geared more toward power napping and reading than Bowflexing and jogging? Then she'd spotted their chariot—a fine candidate for the next makeover on *Pimp My Ride*.

Within moments of collapsing inside the truck— well, she'd collapsed, he was barely even breathing fast—Max had two wires pulled free from beneath the dash. He touched them together and pumped the gas. The second the engine rumbled to life, he rammed it into gear and gunned it. Shockingly, the truck hauled butt and they roared down the road.

Based on his lack of keys, she assumed he was a car thief on top of being a relic-hunting thrill seeker. For a moment she contemplated taking the affronted route, then thought *big whoop*. Ron had worked nine to five doing IT support. A regular paycheck hadn't made him any less of a putz.

Cassie did have a bit of an attitude problem with Max's loaner, though. She sniffed, shifting in her seat and jabbing at the upholstery underneath her leg. "I guess your Mercedes is in the shop?"

He turned south, toward the highway, and checked the rearview mirror. "This isn't mine. I liberated it from the long-term lot at the airport."

She muttered, "And I have no doubt it's been waiting there since 1980 for its owner's return." Trying to find a spot where the seat wasn't actively goosing her, she squirmed around some more and said, "Wasn't there anything better to choose from? Like a Ford Pinto? Or maybe a luxury Pacer?"

Max glanced at the back of his hand, then sucked on a bruised knuckle. "The more expensive the car, the faster it's reported stolen. Police take the recovery more seriously." Shrugging, he added, "The tires are good. The engine's sound. Who cares what it looks like?"

Cassie could only hope that he approached the longevity of his sexual partners with the same practical attitude, and found diminutive stature and an instant addiction to his penis equally as commendable. Based on the fact that they'd already gotten their groove on once, and on his ability to see their vehicle's "inner qualities," this seemed promising.

He winced and stretched his jaw from side to side, assessing the damage. "Don't tell me you're one of those women who judges a guy by what he drives?"

Cassie snorted. "A really sensitive topic for you, I'm sure, given your looks." She had no doubt that he could trot around on the back of a donkey and women would clamor for a chance to ride pillion on his noble steed. "And no, I'm the kind of woman who's lazy and out of shape, and likes her transportation parked within steps of the exit. I'm also the type who hates seat springs poking my rear end when I sit in a vehicle. Especially after running miles just to reach the appalling thing."

Max grunted. "Yeah, well, there were reasons why I didn't leave it running at your front curb."

Yes. He'd been planning to rob her and didn't want

to tip anyone off. Everyone had their pros and cons. Max Stone's just happened to be both.

He held up a hand, clearly anticipating her next question. "Victor's men saw your car in the driveway. They haven't seen this truck. If they do manage to catch up with us, yours would have been too easy to spot."

"Well, the junk-man cover is a winner, let me tell you. We should be safe enough to put everything on hold and take an extended road trip to see America by highway."

Cassie sighed and dropped her head back against the seat. The vinyl was ripped and itched the back of her head, but she didn't bother moving. A nice wide roll of silver tape, the repair item of choice in redneck luxury cruisers like this one, and they'd be set.

Laughing at her previous comeback, he lifted his hand to his face. He prodded at various sore spots, then moved to his ribs. She wanted to cluck and coo over him, but instead gripped the door handle and kept herself glued to her side of the bench seat.

If she started in with the first-aid crap, she'd probably get sidetracked and offer him a medicinal blow job instead. He was still the absolute sexiest thing her ovaries had ever encountered. And she was pathetic.

Max was still chuckling softly. "You're really funny, you know that? Spunky. I like it, but it's gonna get you in trouble one day. Just a warning."

Cassie's mouth pulled flat at the "spunky" comment. "Stop," she said, her voice deadpan. "Next you'll be telling me I have a great personality."

"Hmm." He cocked his head and rubbed his jaw. "I don't know about that. You've been pretty pissy for a while now, peanut. Though I think I know what might cheer you up…." He wiggled his eyebrows, and she forced herself not to pounce on him like a rabid wolverine.

She had no doubt that he was a walking mood elevator, but she was enjoying her grouchiness. It was the only thing keeping her in her pants and off his lap.

She also ignored the "peanut" crack. She was sort of starting to like the obnoxious nicknames he kept using, which showed just how low the horny had fallen. Oh, brother. She was the opposite of pussy whipped. She was dick whipped. Pitiful. Absolutely pitiful.

As they merged onto the main interstate, heading toward Miami, Max flicked his attention to the rearview mirror for the dozenth time.

"Any signs of Huey, Dewey and Louie?" she asked.

"No," he said, the corner of his mouth kicking up. "By the time they dragged themselves off the floor, we were out of there."

"Good. Then we're safe?"

"Yes. More or less. For now, anyway."

Cassie didn't like the sound of that, but planned to address all his cryptic remarks and said, "Then, Lucy, you got some 'splainin' to do. Who the hell is Victor, and why did he send his evil henchmen after my box? For that matter, what sort of man even has evil henchmen?"

She might not be an antiquities expert, but come on. How big a market could there possibly be for a ninety-year-old lover's box, in poor condition, with questionable magical powers in the bedroom? And the Gypsy love charm supposedly only worked if a *woman* used the box, not a man. Oh, yeah, a very hot item. Even if they tried eBay, last year's Beanie Babies would probably bring in higher bids. So what was the deal?

Then Cassie paused. A niggling memory tickled the edges of her thoughts. Something important. A particular word that Max had used back when they were still at her house. A term he'd uttered while he'd brought her to unholy levels of pleasure with nothing more than his wickedly skilled fingers. Some significant remark he'd made that had been sifted to the side while she'd tried to accept that he had only come to steal her lover's box.

Max chuckled, jerking her back to the here and now. "Yep. Spunky," he said. She contemplated slugging him in his battered ribs. Next he'd be calling her feisty. He made her feel like Mighty Mouse.

He also gave those a-mazing orgasms over which she'd earlier rhapsodized, so she said only, "I'm flattered," in a tone that suggested she clearly wasn't. "But enough with the sweet talk. Who's Victor, and why does he want my box?"

He made a face, appearing to be more hassled than angry. As if this Victor guy was a pain in the ass, but one he was used to. "Sworn enemy. He worked for my father, and—" He broke off. "It's not worth going into, believe me. Stupid crap that all started ages ago. It's the longest relationship I've ever been in and I'm ready to break up. He just won't listen when I tell him that we've grown apart and it's time we both moved on."

Cassie grinned in spite of herself. But if he thought that he was going to get away with the short version, then she'd show him "spunky."

Before she could start in with the questions, however, he added as an aside, "And though I realize that we could go back and forth all night on this, it's *my* box. Minerva stole it from me."

"Yes, you've mentioned that," she said, momentarily distracted from the ever-mysterious Victor. "But while we're on the topic, just how exactly did my elderly great-aunt supposedly rob you?" Though, really, Cassie should cut the guy some slack. Minerva was no ordinary woman. Her age was hardly a factor.

Max's expression completely soured, his mouth pulling into a thin line. She couldn't blame him. A dastardly nemesis was probably preferable to Minerva's antics. "Three days ago, I was in a bar in St. Petersburg. I bought the lover's box from this Russian, er…" He frowned and hesitated. His eyes darted toward her, then back to the windshield. "Well, he's sort of like a dealer, or a supplier, really—"

Cassie sighed. "I'm not a Pollyanna. The guy is obviously a fence. The box was probably stolen in the first place. So, go on." She waved her hand.

Max quirked an eyebrow, but continued. "Anyway, I bought the box, then decided to have a few drinks."

"In other words, you were drunk."

"On my way."

"And Minerva tackled you to the ground and stole your box? Wow. She's got skills. Too bad she wasn't here tonight to help you with the fight."

"No. She played up the harmless-old-lady bit and caught me in a weak moment."

"Minerva? A helpless old lady?" Cassie couldn't help snickering.

A muscle started to tick along his jaw. "Hell," he grumbled. "Every hunter on the scene knows Minerva Parker. I was only a kid the first time I saw her in action. Our paths hadn't crossed in years, but when she creaked up to me, all rickety shuffle and stooped posture, I fell for it, figuring she had to be almost a century old by now. Give me a break. It wasn't until I tracked her down, when I went after my box, that she quit the granny act. Then, of course, I had visual proof that she's aged like a flippin' vampire."

Laughing outright, Cassie managed to say, "You're right. Minerva and Lestat. They're both ageless."

Talking over Cassie's latest burst of laughter, Max said, "Enough about the devil-aunt. Bottom line, she stumbled into my bar stool, chattered my ear off and at some point slipped the lover's box from my pack. Probably while I was trying to keep her from breaking a hip," he grumbled.

"Huh. It's not much of a story."

His eyes widening, he shot her an incredulous look. "Do you honestly think I'd make that up?"

Cassie thought about his question for all of a second, then broke into another round of hysterics.

"And would you mind sitting still?" He scowled at her. "One more wiggle and I'm pulling over. Every part of my body aches, including my favorite one, and I'd rather wait till we find a hotel."

Cassie's poor heart had just started to return to a semi-normal rate, and his intimations were like a kick from a pair of cardio paddles. He should yell out "clear" like they did in the E.R. before he started in with the sex stuff.

Frustrated with how quickly the man could arouse her, and admittedly loopy on the hormone rush, she opened her mouth to tell him to knock it off with the fake flirting. Then she promptly closed it, remembering that this would be counterproductive to her goal of fornicating with him as much as humanly possible until he got away.

But pride was vicious evil, and while one portion of her brain was telling her to deep-throat her dignity and do absolutely nothing that might jeopardize her chances of going Kama Sutra with his bad self at the earliest opportunity, another part was saying, *Show some self-respect, girl, he's just using you, yada, yada, yada....*

Well, it was obvious which side was winning and Cassie didn't make a peep.

Meanwhile, Max winced, carefully straightened his left leg and tugged at the seam of his pants. Once he'd gotten everything smoothed out, so to speak, he asked in a casual tone, "So, uh, what exactly did Minerva tell you about the box when she sent it?"

Cassie frowned at him beneath her lashes. He was not so subtly fishing for information, trying to figure out what she knew without sharing anything he didn't have to. *Men,* she thought, turning her head to look out the passenger window. The palmetto trees and scrub brush bordering the highway were a dark, indistinct blur.

She was weighing and discarding various answers when suddenly the hugely important piece of the puzzle—which, a few minutes ago, she'd been racking her brain to remember—popped into her head with all the drama and brilliance of a light switch flipping on a Broadway marquee. Treasure! Max's erotic voice had definitely rasped out the word *treasure*.

"Well," he prompted, his wrist draped across the upper curve of the steering wheel while his thumb tapped out an agitated rhythm. But Cassie barely spared him a glance, just held up her finger in the universal sign for *give me a second*.

Her thoughts were racing. Was the legend of great sex not enough? The box supposedly led to a treasure, too?

Jeez-Louise. She didn't know whether to be impressed or annoyed. At this rate, there was probably a government conspiracy theory lurking around the damned thing, and next the CIA would be gunning for the box. Wait. Scratch that. Minerva had mailed the crappy curio from Russia. Make that the KGB, or whatever they were now called. Wonderful. They were much scarier.

Cassie practically gaped down at the backpack on her lap that held the lover's box inside. What the hell kind of nightmare gift had Minerva sent her? People had been known to kill for treasure!

Meanwhile, Max heaved a sigh of the mightily ag-grieved, and said, "This isn't exactly final *Jeopardy*. I only asked what Minerva told you about the box."

Cassie flipped another finger in Max's direction, one with an entirely different universal sign, and he barked out a laugh. Then she basically ignored him.

Now was not the time to answer any of Max's sneaky, self-serving questions. It was time to figure out what the heck was going on with the lover's box, *then* panic.

Not that she felt all that much like panicking. And if she were being honest, she was more interested than alarmed at the prospect of the box's somehow being linked to a treasure. The danger didn't seem like all that big a deal, and, so far, she'd handled it just fine, and the adventure part sounded way cool, and—

Ack! Cassie stilled, her eyes going wide. The hair on her arms practically stood on end. Okay, she was losing it. Big-time. But she, Cassie Parker—high queen of the wimps—had just used *danger* and *adventure* in the same run-on thought.

Biting her lip, she dug her fingers into the canvas fabric of the backpack. All right. It was too weird, and she'd already been suckered once tonight into believing that the lover's box had made her fantasy come true, but there were certain facts she just couldn't ignore: A) she'd had sex with a tattooed stud who was large and in charge behind his zipper; B) her back somersault, foot to the bad guy's face had been mega kick-ass; C) run-ning for their lives followed by a quick getaway in a

stolen jalopy definitely fell under the *danger* heading;
D) the quest for treasure was about as adventurous as
adventure got; and E) the *excitement* part of the fantasy
had been fulfilled on all levels, cut the recap, enough
said.

Just then Cassie heard a loud *thwock!* and jerked in
her seat. Max had snapped his fingers in front of her
face. "Hey, peanut, you in there? I've been calling your
name for about a minute now."

She frowned at him and batted his hand away. "Don't
do that. And before you rupture a spleen or something,
yes, yes, I know about the treasure." She shrugged, as
blasé as if she were talking about meat loaf for dinner.

Some newfound instinct told her to play the whole
scene casual, and she went with it. Besides, as neat-o
as the whole secret treasure thing might be, she was far
more concerned about the truly important things in
life—like did the Gypsy sex charm really work, thus
giving her the power to fulfill her rapacious carnal
hungers whenever struck by whim, or was she the
victim of placebo Gypsy magic?

Admittedly, not the first snag that most people would
need cleared up, but what could she say.

Max cursed and banged the heel of his hand against
the steering wheel. "Of course, the devil-aunt told you
about the treasure. I don't know why I bothered asking,"
he griped. "As we speak, she's probably mouthing off
to some asshole back in St. Petersburg, just waiting to
join the chase."

Only halfway paying attention to his rant, Cassie

made a sort of neutral grunt. Who knew what the heck Minerva was doing? And who cared? She couldn't be bothered with all that right now, and needed to figure out whether or not she had access to occult powers that would make her every kinky dream come true. She'd worry about the stupid treasure later.

Obviously, there was only one way to know for sure if the lover's box was under a Gypsy sex spell. She needed to write another fantasy. And it needed to be a doozy. None of that generic stuff. Cassie needed to come up with something daring…something exotic…something that would rule out pity sex, yet not drag in barnyard animals.

She spotted a billboard advertising a cheap hotel coming up in a few miles. Perfect. They needed a room. And she needed a pen and some privacy to remove her nipple ring, unlock the box and fill in the next page of her diary.

"So we're safe now, right? No chance of any big bad guys finding us?"

Max had still been bitching about Minerva when she'd interrupted, and he broke off and asked, "Huh?"

"I mean it's safe to stop, right? Maybe find a place to sleep for the rest of the night? It's so late and I'm really, really tired…." Giving an exaggerated yawn, she started shifting in her seat and wiggling her hips. In slow-mo, with a lip lick and a hair toss thrown in for good measure. Then she pointed up ahead. "I saw a sign and we can get a room at the next exit. What do you think?"

Max did a double take while the truck swerved. Then he nodded his head and flipped on the turn signal.

6

CASSIE UNLOCKED THE LOVER'S BOX. In the background she could hear the water running from the hotel room's dinky shower while Max washed off random smears of blood and accompanying grime earned during his earlier fight. Meanwhile, she'd pretty much exhausted her powers of imagination picturing him naked, soapy and wet. Hubba-hubba… But she had things to do before he finished up and came back into the room, and she needed to get busy.

She'd already wasted too much time fluffing her hair, slipping off her clothes, then wrapping herself in one of the bedsheets as if it were the latest in lingerie-inspired fashion.

Cassie snagged the plastic pen from the bedside table, then turned her diary to the second page. The problem was that she had no more idea of what to scribble down as the next installment in Cassie Parker's Wild and Woolly Sex Diary than she'd had earlier tonight.

Except that instead of being in her bedroom with a glass of wine and all the time in the world to come up with something nifty, she was stuck in the roach motel and had five minutes tops before Max Stone hopped out of the shower and caught her trying to use Gypsy voodoo to get him in the sack.

In other words, Cassie had around three-hundred seconds to come up with something kinky enough to be outside the realm of normal sex yet tame enough that if the Gypsy sex charm actually worked Cassie had something left to try that didn't involve a leather-clad dominatrix with a scary German accent and a paddle.

Cripes. *What to write…what to write…?* Her gaze darted to the flimsy bathroom door while she tapped her pen in a spastic beat on the glaringly blank white page.

Okay, she told herself. Forget fancy and exotic. She was a washout in the kinky department. Apparently her imagination had no natural middle ground between missionary position with a real, live male and absurd porno stereotypes. Bottom line, she needed to figure out what sort of sexual acts, whether tame or depraved, her body craved to enact with Max Stone if given another chance, then start writing.

Well, duh, that was easy. With the über-hottie as her muse, she immediately had her answer, and almost pumped her fist in the air and shouted out ye-e-e-es!

Cassie promptly put pen to paper. She wanted full access to Max Stone's totally naked body anywhere and anytime she desired. She wanted the power to merely think about him in the buff and he would strip down, ready and raring to go.

Okay, so she wanted to work through some of her

leftover issues. In hindsight, and with her hate goggles firmly in place, Cassie could now see just how selfish a lover Ron had been. Sex had been at his initiation, and he'd turned her down more times than any woman's self-esteem should ever have to endure. Of course, on the rare, rare (had she mentioned rare) occasions when Ron had wanted it, she'd been expected to drop everything and immediately assume whatever position he was in the mood for.

Now, to some, this might not seem as self-esteem devouring as she knew it to be. However, trust her on this one, it was a lulu. Becoming a caricature of Mrs. Roper from *Three's Company* crossed with Peg Bundy from *Married with Children* whenever Cassie wanted some lovin' was the mental equivalent of bathing suit shopping with Pamela Anderson every day for a year. There wasn't enough positive thinking in the world to get over that kind of head game.

Cassie had fallen for the beta, nice-guy crap Ron had faked at the beginning of their relationship, and hadn't seen him for the demon-sucking font of evil he really was until it was too late. Which just made her feel like even more of a loser.

Well, no more. Cassie had no idea how long any of this would last with Max, but it was her one chance, and as long as she was testing the lover's box, she was going to write down what she really and truly desired.

She wanted Max and his sexuality wide open and at her disposal. Especially his body. It fascinated her. He fascinated her, and she wanted to pose his nude length, then lick, and kiss and bite him anywhere and everywhere she pleased. She wanted him to masturbate in front of her, and to watch him climax. She wanted to lie back and have him climb up her until his knees rested by her shoulders, and then she wanted him to slide that huge, hard cock of his deep into her mouth.

She wanted anything-goes sex—no shyness, no balking, nothing but pure excitement. The more revealing her requests, the more aroused he would become. Total access whenever and however she wanted.

Pretty darn pleased with herself, she locked the diary inside the lover's box. She returned the little key to the thin gold hoop, lowering the sheet and sliding her nipple ring back into place. And right then, the moment she got the ring onto her breast, she heard the shower cut off. Her eyes wide, she turned her head toward the bathroom while the tiny key at her nipple practically vibrated and sent an erotic pulse of heat spreading across her skin.

Cassie's voice was a froggy croak as she whispered, "No flippin' way…."

AFTER TEN MINUTES of freezing cold water pounding away at him, Max's brain was finally a little clearer. Oh, he still wanted Cassie Parker, all right, more than he'd ever wanted another woman. All that was the same, just with the painful edge of urgency mercifully eased. He could at least think around his desire. A decided improvement over his physical condition for the last couple of hours. Bizarre and admittedly scary as hell, but there you had it.

Of course, his good buddy was still hanging a little too stiff and thick for Max's liking, and that was after jacking off the second he'd stepped under the water. For now he ignored the eager thing, even the minimal relief better than nothing. And hopefully, by taking the matter in hand, so to speak, he wouldn't embarrass himself with the whole speed issue as he had earlier.

Hell. At the memory of how quickly he'd been ready to come the minute he'd slid inside the goddess, a flash of heat scored his cheekbones. He felt about sixteen years old. And the feeling sucked. It really did.

From the moment he'd clapped eyes on Cassie Parker he'd been following a whole new set of instincts and none of them made sense. Neither his thoughts nor his actions. Any second he expected the theme song to *The Twilight Zone* to start playing in the background.

To say that he was acting out of character by plotting all the different ways he could go at the goddess like a horny jackrabbit rather than just taking the lover's box and ditching her the first chance he got was the understatement of the century.

Not to mention that his jackrabbit plan shouldn't even be an option no matter how smokin' hot she was. Hell, her great-aunt had stolen the lover's box from him once already. For all he knew, the goddess was in cahoots with her sticky-fingered relative and was just biding her time before she tried to sneak off and go after the treasure herself.

Even worse than his chronic boner and his general indifference to his start date for finding the Gypsy king's riches was the realization that he genuinely *liked* Cassie Parker. A lot. Found her fascinating. Every shocking thing she did, and every smart-ass word she uttered. In his experience, this was unheard of.

He, Max Stone, was completely smitten. Twitter-pated. The victim of a schoolboy crush. Well, a grown-up, highly pornographic crush, anyway. And the more she chattered at him, the worse it got. She cracked him up. Which almost scared him more than the rest combined. Any female who made him want to laugh and come at the same time was one dangerous woman. And he preferred his danger of the life-or-death variety. Not the leash-around-his-prick variety. That he'd most likely already had the line snapped on, with a gal the size of Tinker Bell pulling the lead, should have him freaking right the hell out. But it wasn't.

Now, contrary to his present behavior, he wasn't a total moron and he had his suspicions about what this meant. However, soul mate and love at first sight were concepts he'd always mentally filed away under the heading, Shit To Be Avoided. Max was just plain not up to dealing with the dilemma of his feelings right this very second.

He'd ponder all that freaky crap later. Like in forty-eight hours or so, after he'd completed his horny-jack-rabbit plan. Then he would do what any normal man would—sensibly ignore his scary-ass feelings toward the teacup goddess, then get his box and get the hell out. After, of course, making sure that Victor was aware of the fact that Cassie Parker was completely out of the hunt for the treasure, and that he'd hang Vic's balls from his rearview mirror if his goons ever went near Cassie again. And after, of course, he also made sure that Cassie understood that he was not going to be dicked around by the Parker women anymore.

A couple of days of no-holds-barred sex, and he'd be back in control and back in the game. But the idea of being back in control and back in the game didn't cheer him up like it should. And he was scared as hell he knew why.

Aware that there was probably a full-blown scowl on his face, Max flipped open the tiny bottle, then shampooed his hair. Moving his hands through the lather and trying to think about absolutely nothing, he suddenly stilled and every muscle in his body went tense. His tattoo, even with the cool water spraying over his skin, started throbbing with pulses of heat.

His damn cock, which had finally fallen to half-mast, lengthened in stiff jerks until he was hard enough to cut diamonds. Just like that, Max was desperate and dying to be back inside Cassie. Now. And before he had any real idea what he was doing, he quickly rinsed his hair then turned off the spray.

He flung back the plastic curtain, the metal hooks whirring along the steel rod. He was pulled by an overwhelming compulsion. Cassie wanted him—needed him—urgently, and he needed to be there for her. He didn't know how he knew, he just did.

Dripping water in little puddles, he started reaching for a towel, then hesitated. Somehow, it just seemed like a bad idea… Then he thought, *screw it,* pulled open the door and strode into the bedroom.

"OHMYGOSH, ohmygosh, ohmygosh" Cassie muttered, feeling her eyes go impossibly wide when she spotted Max.

She held up her hand and managed to say, "Wait." Her thoughts were a jumbled mess. His striding out like a wet, naked warrior was too much to be a fluke. Nothing made sense.

He immediately paused while she gaped. She wanted to wave her hand toward him like a magician's assistant—ta-da! All she could think was, *look at him. Just look at him. The absolutely sexiest human in existence. And he's mine. All mine. Until he robs me and takes off, I get to play with him at will. Yippee! Yeah! Yahoo!*

Cassie Parker had never seen anything like Max Stone going full monty for her own private viewing pleasure. He was magnificent. He was…heck, adjectives hadn't yet been invented that would do him justice.

His beautiful, almost shoulder-length hair, with its rainbow of colors from warm browns to antique golds, was now wet and slicked darkly to his head.

His piercing blue-green eyes were heavy-lidded and bright—the ultimate bedroom eyes. His nose was narrow and straight. Well, normally it was. Now, the bridge was puffy and red from where one of the goons had gotten in a punch. Yet this didn't detract from the overall picture. The bruises that shadowed his jaw and cheekbone, and those marring his ribs, could have been applied by a master artist. They drew the eye toward his masculine lines and somehow highlighted the perfection of bone and muscle as if he were the very essence of man, beautiful yet wounded in battle. The ultimate warrior.

The symmetry of his features, his entire face and form were, well…in her opinion, Max Stone was the standard by which all men should be judged. Enough said. It was too much, really, for one poor pair of eyeballs to take in.

She could see his Adam's apple bob while he swallowed, the small movement filled with tension. Beads of water dripped down his sculpted torso, and his nipples were puckered tight against his damp, glistening skin. Any chill he might be feeling, however, was not affecting his *massive* erection.

Yeesh. When the lover's box delivered, it some kind of delivered….

His voice a husky rumble, he said, "Tell me what you want. Anything. Everything. Just don't hold me off."

She stared, the sight dizzying. "No," she managed. "I would never hold you off." And, boy, was that the truth. *Yep.* She was going insane. Because the lover's box must really work. The evidence was too great to ignore.

She would never normally be able to flip on every tacky lamp in the room so as not to miss a single glorious inch of his manly perfection. She would have felt too awkward or embarrassed. But not now. Not tonight…

As she'd turned up the lights, Max's gaze had

followed her every action. He stood in the center of the carpet, sopping wet from head to toe, his hands spreading wide, then fisting. He looked like he was on display, an artist's model, or a living human-anatomy lesson.

His diabolically sexy tattoo curved from halfway down his taut buttock, over and around his hip, to spread across the front of his groin and pubic area on the left side. One of the dragon's claws arched onto his thigh, the other reached toward his thick cock. Lordy, lordy, the man had it going on.

She could practically hear her heart pounding. The power rushing through every capillary in her body almost made her sway on her feet. Watching him, especially his engorged shaft, she ached for release. She felt no awkwardness or conflicting emotion, only anticipation.

As if he'd spoken in her mind, she knew that he wanted nothing more than to give her pleasure. Anything she requested. Everything she wanted from him and more, fantasies she hadn't even thought of yet. All for her satisfaction, the culmination of her desires.

"What are you waiting for?" his voice grated. "Tell me what to do…."

Her own voice husky, she whispered, "Touch yourself. Stroke your cock like you do when you're alone and no one's watching."

His nostrils flared and he cursed, but his hand went to his length as if pulled by a magnet. As soon as he clasped himself, he made a broken sound. He squeezed his eyes tightly shut and she could see him grit his teeth, his jaw clenching.

His erection strained, the head dark red. He clamped his hand tightly, then slowly slid along his shower-dampened flesh to the thick knob at the top. Then, as if waiting to make sure that she didn't miss a second of his progress, he slightly eased his firm grip and unhurriedly slipped back downward until the side of his wrist touched the dense nest of hair at his base.

Then he did it again. And again…and again…

As he methodically worked his fist up, the center vein would press flat, then rush full on each measured downstroke. He knew his own rhythm, what he liked, and she could feel a gush of moist heat trickle between her legs.

She stepped closer, mesmerized, her clitoris throbbing with its own pulse. She stood at his side, her breath coming in quick gasps that matched his as she watched. Thick tears of pearly fluid rained from the tip, adding a wet, clicking sound every time he'd glide his fist, deliberate and firm, over the ridge at the head of his penis.

Somehow she found her voice and said, "Move your feet apart a little more. I want your legs wider."

His eyelids flew up and his stunning blue-green gaze latched on to hers. She froze, the moment painfully intimate. Arousing beyond anything she'd experienced. His large, chiseled thighs flexed as if he fought her request yet had no choice but to obey, and he shifted his stance.

She reached out, bringing her hand to his flank. He hissed in a breath and lost his rhythm. His tattoo, the beautiful ink design that she found so, so delicious and fascinating, was incredibly warm beneath her palm.

She almost expected it to move and writhe beneath her fingers, the artwork stunning and hypnotic.

Her hands trembling, she reached up and jerked open the knot of her makeshift robe. It fell to the ground but she barely noticed. She couldn't look away from the slow, hypnotic pumps along his length, and she pressed herself to his side, rubbing her breasts against the thick muscles of his arm. The contact made him flinch.

"Shit…" He muttered the curse, over and over, clearly fighting not to change the pace he'd set.

The muscles in his stomach contracted, then heaved in and out with his bellowing lungs, and he started fisting his shaft faster, stronger. With his stance wider, she pressed her mound against the side of his upper thigh and hip, widening her own thighs and letting her wet flesh drag and glide, her curls and damp center sliding against his skin, rubbing herself against him.

His whole body stiffened and his cursing grew more inventive and louder. He locked his knees, keeping a firm stance that she couldn't rock off balance, his hand now mercilessly stroking his arousal.

She rose up on the balls of her feet and she whispered directly in his ear while she worked herself to orgasm, "I'm going to really touch you now, and you're going to let me."

He growled out a vicious sound and, again, speared her with his lightning-hot gaze. Their eyes locked together, she slid her hand down over his world-class backside, lower and lower. If possible, his length shot harder, his entire cock a deep, angry red as she slipped her fingers beneath to the smooth skin behind his sack. His testicles were pulled up tight to his body. He was going to go off any second.

She fondled and painstakingly explored everything she could reach. He started shaking, a juddering sound breaking behind his teeth. Making a little pincher between her forefinger and thumb, she rubbed and pinched the ridge of skin between his puckered flesh and his swaying bulge. Back and forth, over and over, with a slow twist of her wrist.

On and on, she watched and stared, moved and touched. Too much, too much, and Cassie found herself begging, "Please…"

Proving that he could wrestle control at any time, but had willingly handed her the reins, he said, "Please what…?" The words were practically torn from his throat they sounded so harsh.

"Come. Now," she panted.

"Then watch. Everything…"

As Cassie stared, Max's nostrils flared and his stomach contracted and right as her inner muscles convulsed and clamped down painfully, his penis jerked in his hand and he shot into the air, jet after jet of creamy fluid pulsing with each beat of his release. She could feel his climax beneath her fingers, his internal muscles giving one hard twitch after another, and she unbelievably came again as Max spent himself right into the air. Wide open, nothing hidden, every beat of his body and emotion racing across his face, his hips bucking forward and the swing of his heavy testicles bumping against the back of her hand and fingers.

It was beautiful, stunning, and she threw her free arm around his chest, keeping herself from dropping in a puddle to the floor.

Max wiped his hand against his stomach, rubbing the viscous fluid against his skin, making the ribbed bands of muscle shine. Then he turned and held her up, his strength awesome, as he whispered into her hair, "That was great, shortstuff. So what's next?"

7

BY THE NEXT MORNING, Max didn't think that there was a licensed physician on the planet who'd ever examined his bare body as attentively and thoroughly as had the tiny temptress. He'd have felt violated if he weren't so busy being grateful.

He'd been posed, viewed, touched, fondled, kissed, suckled and bitten in every possible spot where those things could be done. He'd come so hard and so many times that he wouldn't be surprised if she'd trained his sex to perform for her at will. Voice commands, hand signals, you name it and he'd respond to it as if she was the one giving the orders.

Hours earlier, when they'd finally fallen into bed—back when he'd been spraddled across the sheets and she'd all but devoured him whole—her variation on sixty-nine had been so mind-blowing he could have died right there and been a happy man. Every time he touched her it was too good to be true. Almost surreal. The two of them together approached the stuff of fantasies.

Their hotel stay had been phenomenal, and they

hadn't even gotten around to intercourse. She'd had him use his own hands on his body, then her hands on his body, then her mouth on his body, then let him try his mouth on her body at the same time…. Hell, as amazing as it all had been, they really hadn't known each other long enough to be bored with the basics yet, and he was actually starting to crave a shot at straight missionary.

When a guy was starting to dream about good old-fashioned, plain vanilla sex just for a change of pace—and he'd known his partner for less than twenty-four hours, yet had sustained a practically constant erection in her presence like he was freebasing Viagra—well then, he was obviously on to something that was too good to let go of anytime soon. He might have just found himself a keeper.

Max sat up in the bed and swung his legs to the side, dropping his elbows to his knees. He stared absently at the wall and slowly shook his head. Yep, fate must be busting a gut and he plain didn't care, because he was…well, because he was *content* in a way he'd never been in his entire life. The constant restlessness that drove him was strangely stilled. Corny as it sounded, he felt as if he was finally coming home after being away too long.

Aw, crap. A woman he lo—, er, liked and some fantastic sex and he was blathering to himself like a sappy greeting card. Max immediately cut off the mushy thoughts. After all those orgasms, and the damn near perfect female who'd been responsible for them, he was in too fine a mood to ruin it by thinking about stupid stuff like his feelings.

All in all, regardless of the raging drive to bone her, if he quit it with the Hallmark junk, then he was back in control. His goals were clear: mate with the goddess until his body was one step from hospitalization, make sure Victor and his men were never a threat to her again, then go after the treasure.

There. That sounded good. Mostly. He'd just have to send his Johnson a memo when the time came.

Max yawned and rubbed his face. He could hear Cassie in the bathroom. She was humming something horrendous and off-key. It sounded suspiciously like the theme song from *Raiders of the Lost Ark*. He almost laughed out loud. *Yep.* She was dangerous as hell.

Smiling, no doubt like a buffoon, he walked over to his duffel bag. He bypassed his clothes. For some reason, every time he thought about getting dressed he just…couldn't. But he shrugged this off. Naked was easier, anyway, where the goddess was concerned.

He reached for his cell phone, then checked the bars on the screen. He had a full battery and he had satellite access. Technology was a wonderful thing. Since Max rarely stayed in one place for long, an international cell service was a must-have.

While he had a breather before Cassie came back into the bedroom and he was put to stud again, he needed to touch base with a couple of his contacts back in Russia. Even though he planned to lie low for a day or two, and let Cassie put him through his paces, it wouldn't hurt to start spreading the word that the box was back in his possession.

The faster Victor heard, the faster Cassie would no longer be a target. He'd only let her carry the lover's box in her pack because it was easier than arguing and it suited his more lustful purposes to keep her docile. On some level, she had to know that he could walk away with the shoddy antique anytime he wanted.

And while he was at it, it wouldn't hurt to put out a few feelers to see how Victor was handling the fact that Max had beaten him to the Gypsy king's box, again, then beat up his men. Not that Victor was a concerned employer. He simply loved to thwart Max and usually went ape whenever he failed.

Ten minutes later, however, and Max was the one ready to go primal….

"ARE YOU SURE THE DIARY is really that important to finding this, um, treasure stuff?" Cassie asked, trying to appear as if the loss of Stasi's diary was only a small setback, as well as appear knowledgeable about the whole treasure issue. Or at least not clueless on the topic. This wasn't going so well for her.

Unfortunately, she'd never given the other woman's diary another thought once she'd shoved it away inside her closet.

His jaw clenched hard enough that a muscle was bulging along the edge, Max gave a choppy, "Yes. Pretty important."

A few moments ago Max had roared her name repeatedly, she'd raced out of the bathroom like it was on fire, and then he'd loudly shared with her the details of his phone call. The basic gist of his lecture-a-thon was that Max had just contacted some of his associates—people like himself who played the black market like a bunch of eBay sellers. According to his cohorts in crime, word on the street was that Victor's men had Stasi's diary and he had set up a private sale for tomorrow night. Which meant that the goons had ransacked her bedroom after Cassie and Max had left, and were taking the dang thing to St. Petersburg.

Talk about hitting another snag.

Even worse, Cassie had no idea what the treasure was, any of the legend that connected this hidden wealth to the lover's box, or how Stasi's diary was supposed to help someone find it. Oh, or why this Victor fella was such an asshole.

Minerva hadn't even mentioned the treasure when she'd sent Cassie the box. Well, that, or Cassie had been so distracted by all the making-her-sex-fantasies-come-true stuff that she'd missed everything else. But that didn't seem likely. Yes, she was lonely and desperate, but she was greedy, too. Reading about a treasure would've at least earned a mental footnote.

Cassie ignored the fact that Max was magnificently angry and eyeing her like a horny python who wanted to strangle her and screw her at the same time. She'd somehow managed to drag her clothes on while he'd been yelling at her earlier, and she now walked to her backpack, tossed her makeup bag inside and took out her brush.

Her face warmed. She'd remembered makeup, hair

gel and birth control pills but had completely forgotten Stasi's diary. Apparently, she hadn't matured past high school. Put her around a hot guy and her priorities turned to beauty aids and contraceptives. Still blushing, she took a quick peek at Max, then thought *Screw maturity*. She defied any woman not to primp around that hunk.

She stood in front of the mirror hanging above the room's one shabby dresser and started brushing out her hair. "I don't understand why Victor would want to sell the diary."

Max's expression turned menacing. "He's an idiot, so I don't always have a complete handle on his motivations. But at a guess, I'd say there are a few possibilities. One, he's trying to smoke me out. Either to see if I'll offer him some kind of trade for the diary or because he plans to ambush me, steal the box and go after the treasure himself. Two, he's just a mean-spirited son of a bitch and would sell the diary and ruin his own chances of getting the treasure just to make sure I don't get it, either. Or three, someone's willing to pay a whole hell of a lot of money for the diary, and they've made Victor an offer he can't refuse. My money's on the ambush theory, but I could be wrong."

Cassie said something clever like, "Gluck," then cleared her throat. She'd caught the basic gist of his assessment but, since he was naked and his diabolically sexy tattoo had been all but winking at her and crooking one of its clever claws in her direction with the distinct suggestion of *would you like to pet me or hop on my back for a quick ride,* she wasn't at her deductive best.

Cassie bolstered the impression that she was a complete ninny by ignoring the importance of his explanation. Instead, she said, "Umm, would you…er…uh…mind maybe putting some clothes on?"

Her request didn't exactly improve his temperament and he gritted out, "I can't. I've tried." He shook his head, his expression a mix of bafflement and exasperation.

This time Cassie's face more than warmed. It flamed. Apparently, even when she wasn't trying, she was a total horn dog. "Oh. Well. You might want to try again. I have a feeling it'll work this time."

Max threw up his hands and shook his head. "Whatever." He marched to his duffel bag and pulled out a clean pair of cargos. He looked mildly surprised when he was actually able to step into them.

Watching him, it was all Cassie could do not to grin smugly and rub her hands together. These little reminders of just how well the box worked were coo-wel. And they made her all the more determined to hang on to the silly-looking antique no matter the cost.

Victor would have to rip the Gypsy king's box from her kung-fu grip, then step over her dead and prone body if he hoped to steal it. There was no way in hell she was giving up Max Stone or the Gypsy relic/sex toy.

But Cassie still didn't understand how the diary was supposed to help them find a treasure. "You know, I pretty much read the entire diary that Rajko's lover wrote. Sometimes she went by Krasili, but she mostly signed her stuff as Stasi. And unless Stasi used a complex code of various sexual positions for keys on a map, then I don't see how her journal would lead anyone to a treasure."

Max had been reaching for his shirt. He stilled. "Is that all this Stasi wrote about?"

Cassie hesitated, mentally squirming. She really didn't want to touch this one with a ten-foot pole. So far, Max hadn't said a word about the sexual fantasy stuff and, if he didn't already know, then the last thing she wanted to do was spill the beans. Not to mention that it was her own diary presently locked inside Rajko's box and the reason for his insatiable attitude where she was concerned.

Hoping her expression was suitably filled with lust for mysterious treasure and not his shag-u-licious bod, she tried to sound discouraged. "Yep. Just page after page of how much she loved her Gypsy rescuer, then on and on about what she dreamed of doing to and with him now that they were together."

He zeroed in on one of her words. "Rescuer?"

She shrugged. "Stasi doesn't go into specifics, but she gives the impression that Rajko saved her life. That he was her hero." Cassie waved her hand. "You know, romantic stuff like how she would've died if he hadn't found her and now that he had, she'd die if she couldn't do him morning, noon and night. But nothing about a stash of gold bars, or Spanish doubloons. And I would have noticed a map of an island with a big *X* at Dead-Man's Cave, if I'd seen it. I don't understand why you and this Victor think Stasi's diary is so important."

That was the least of what she didn't understand, but it was a good starting place.

Max barked out a laugh. "You got the wrong scene playing in your mind, shortstuff. Minerva should have given you a better debriefing."

True. Minerva's debriefing had stuck to one topic and it hadn't been treasure.

"Rajko wasn't a pirate off the Barbary Coast. Forget Black Bart or Captain Hook with a map and a big *X*." Chuckling, he shook his he head. "Though I did think *Tinker Bell* when I first saw you, so I guess you can't help it."

Must he make her feel like an actual pygmy? And she looked nothing like Tinker Bell. But since the four-inch-tall cartoon character was more hot than not, Cassie supposed there were worse comparisons, and, instead of killing him, she only stuck out her tongue, then said, "Shut up. Seriously. You're being a pain."

He grinned. "And you're seriously cute." Then he grabbed her and planted a quick, toe-curling kiss on her mouth. *Do not picture him naked, do not picture him naked,* she chanted to herself while she gasped for air. It must have worked, because Max finished dressing and went on with his mini history lesson.

"We're talking jewels, peanut. A czar's ransom worth, according to legend. Think Russia before the revolution. Filthy-rich aristocrats dripping furs and jewels, and starving, barefoot peasants in the balmy snow."

Please. Cassie was female, she liked romance novels

and she'd read Susan Johnson's early works, so she immediately caught the vision. But she didn't want to interrupt, and merely nodded and twirled her hand in a *hurry up* motion. Fortunately, her faux pas on the type of treasure they were after seemed to have mellowed his earlier mad-on and loosened his tongue.

"And as far as this Stasi woman's diary is concerned, nobody knows whether it's important or not. That's the whole point. Most historians don't even think the box existed, let alone that Rajko really had a treasure. Right or wrong, Gypsies were known for stealing and fortune-telling. Not for amassing wealth. When my old man was alive, he was one of the few people who believed Rajko's lover was the secret to the legend—that the treasure was probably hers. It was also one of the few original theories he ever had. He normally wasn't one to disagree with popular academic thought."

Though Max had sounded totally indifferent when he'd mentioned his father, she paused. Cassie might not know her own father—men never fared well with the Parker gals—but she empathized with his loss. Also, she wanted a peek inside Max's head. "Oh, I'm sorry your dad passed away. Has it been long?"

He shot her a funny look. "Oka-a-ay. A bit off topic. But, uh, no, it's fine. He died a while ago. And we were never what you would call close. My mom died when I was a kid, and he started taking me with him on his digs. There was no place else to dump me and money was tight. Any extra went toward his excavations. At the time I didn't know any better and wanted to go with him. But, he…uh…" Max stared at the floor, one hand tugging on his ear. "When I was little I have a few memories of him being nice. Laughing."

Cassie nodded encouragingly, not daring to interrupt. "I don't know when it changed. He just could never be wrong. About anything. Except he wasn't really all that bright," he continued. "I mean, yeah, he was a professor, but it was all book smarts. He didn't have much imagination. Couldn't make leaps with his reasoning and stuck with documented theories. I used to argue with him. I saw things he didn't. Had better instincts. Then I'd be right and he'd go ape-shit. Ugly crap. Since there was no way to get rid of me, he'd eventually make like my ideas had been his from the beginning. Finally it wasn't an act. He'd really believe it." Max stopped and wrinkled his forehead. "Why are we talking about this?"

She totally ignored his last remark, fascinated by this flash into his personal life, and said, "He must have been, well, less than thrilled that you ended up playing on the other side." She was referring to the well-known rivalry between the academic community and hunters who learned their skills in the field, like Max and her great-aunt.

Max shrugged. "He accused me of robbing graves long before I ever got started. It bothered me when I was younger, but I'm fine with how I live and don't usually waste my time worrying about what people think. You know, have you ever considered Ritalin? Talking with you is like verbal ADD. What was I saying before?"

Cassie knew he felt awkward sharing as much as he

had. It wasn't the time to push for more. So she pretended to be annoyed at his insult and said with a sniff, "Try to keep up. Russia. Your father. His theories about Rajko's girlfriend."

"Oh, sorry." He smirked, sliding his feet into his hiking boots, then sitting on the side of the bed and lacing them up. "My fault entirely. I'll try to keep pace."

He ignored her eye roll and said, "Anyway, Rajko and this Stasi would've been making their booty calls at the height of the war. Based on what my dad said, he'd come across a little-known story about the diary. Something to do with the Gypsy king and his lover. Whatever it was, he didn't believe it. Thought it was a smoke screen."

Max gave a small frown, then shook his head. "At the time, we weren't getting along so well and he didn't share the details with me. But whatever he'd heard made him think that the woman who wrote the diary would've had to be educated. Not a peasant.

"One option was that she was some bored count's wife and, when the revolution came her way, she took the family jewels, then split to be with her Gypsy lover. Another was that she'd grown up in one of the royal households. Probably the child of a favored upper servant who was educated with the princesses. As an adult she'd have been a lady's maid or companion at the czar's summer palace. My dad theorized that when the Bolsheviks hit, she stole a few royal 'trinkets' during the confusion and took off with her Gypsy boy toy." Max stood, then shrugged again.

"Nobody knows. But I will. That's what relic hunters

do. Find the facts buried inside the fables so that they can find the relic. But since my dad thought Rajko's lover was the key, and Victor used to work for my dad, then, yes, the diary is important. Vic and I both know it."

Cassie merely stared as Max started picking up his dirty clothes from where he'd dropped them on the floor last night and shoved them into his duffel bag. She was hugely relieved. Obviously, though Max's father had heard about the sexual-fantasy aspect of the box's legend, he'd blown it off as ridiculous and hadn't bothered to share the details with his son. Which meant that her secret was still safe and Max didn't have a clue that she was using occult powers to have her wicked way with him. Phew!

She was speechless. Barbary pirates? Bolsheviks? Russian Revolution? Max knew about all that stuff, and not from steamy novels. Damn. Otherworldly handsomeness, unholy levels of sex appeal and a brain, too. That's it. Cassie was marrying him now. She'd have him wrestled into a pair of Dockers and driving a minivan in no time.

Wait. Forget that. She was done with that kind of guy. They were merely jerks in dorks' clothing.

Besides, she didn't want to change Max. Well, mostly, she didn't. Sure, the lover's box may have made her brave and adventurous, but she still had a uterus, so, *of course* she wanted to tweak his habits a little. Just on the important things. Like monogamy, and maybe writing a fantasy where Mr. Tall, Gorgeous and Tattooed was struck impotent with anyone except her. *Note to self, jot that down and lock it inside the lover's box ASAP.*

She'd also like to soothe Max's inner demons. Come on, the man had "brooding with inner pain that only the right woman could heal" written all over him. And after hearing about his butthead father, it wasn't hard to figure out why.

And she wanted the treasure. Hey, a bunch of jewels sounded très exciting and she wouldn't mind being rich as well as sexually powerful.

Wow. Cassie had a kinky new sex life and she actually wanted to hunt for treasure. Apparently, Oprah and Dr. Phil were barking up the wrong tree. The key to personal growth wasn't found inside oneself; Gypsy magic was the way to go!

While Max shuffled around the room, brushing his teeth and getting ready, she couldn't help but remember the last time she'd made a foray into the archeology world. It had been during college break, freshman year. She'd tripped over a shovel lying around the excavation site, fallen on the remnant of an ancient clay bowl— circa the rein of Queen Tuten-Titmouse that had been earlier unearthed, then crushed it to smithereens with her big fat backside. Minerva had never nagged her into helping again. And Cassie had given up all hope of being like the other infamous Parker gals and promptly changed her major to business.

Well, all those nasty little hang-ups seemed to have gone bye-bye, and it was time to go adventurin'. She and Max had some arch-enemy butt to kick, and a diary to get back.

Cassie clapped her hands together, and boomed like a locker-room coach, "Okey-dokey. We better stop dawdling. We need to swing by my house and get my passport before we flee the country, and the clock's ticking." Then she added under her breath, "And rope the poor kid next door into feeding Creature." But she was in too good a mood to work up much annoyance over her great-aunt's crazy cat.

She walked to the wobbly desk propped in the corner, and lifted the lover's box. She'd never gotten a chance to put it away after she'd written out her second fantasy and Max had come storming out of the shower, all wet, and naked, and hard, and they'd— *Whoops, do not go there. The poor man had just gotten his clothes on.*

Max noticed what she was holding, and started. "Cripes, woman. You just left it sitting out again?" He snatched the box from her hands, towering over her. "What is wrong with you? What if Victor's men had followed us? The minute they broke into the room, they'd have had it."

"Oh, lighten up, you big baby. Like you'd have let them snatch the lover's box—*not*. But from now on I'll make sure I hide it in my super-safe backpack, where no one would ever dream of looking." She held out her hand and wiggled her fingers. "Now give me the box and I'll put it away. Times a' wasting and we've gotta make tracks."

The vertically blessed jerk held the box over her head like he was in the third grade and they were playing Keep Away. "*We* don't have to go anywhere. I think I've told you this already, but Rajko's box is mine. And I'm going after the diary by myself. It's too dangerous. You will hang out somewhere safe for a few days. Victor will forget all about you, and I—"

"And *you* are an asshole," she finished for him. "Also, you're wrong. It's your word against Minerva's over who owns the lover's box. We'll zip by her hotel room once we get to St. Petersburg. If you two can't agree and make nice, then we'll go after the treasure together and split it fifty-fifty." In Cassie's opinion, this sounded a heck of a lot better than the truth, which was something more along the lines of—*Yeah, yeah, there's a good possibility that my wacky great-aunt stole the box from you. But I'm not done using the Gypsy sex charm to boink your brains out and I think a fortune of antique jewels will perfectly accessorize my fall wardrobe. And you'll look nice on my arm, too. Nice and naked...*

The man seemed to have only two facial expressions when he glared at her: horny or harassed. Oh, and angry. Right now he was wearing the middle one. "Listen. You and I both know that there's nothing you can do to stop me from taking Rajko's box and hitting the road. I was hoping to lie low with you for a few days, but now that Victor has the diary, it's no longer an option. Believe me, the last thing I want to do is walk away from you and this bed."

"Stop. You're getting me all misty eyed." But Cassie really wasn't as peeved as she'd sounded. Other than the party pack of orgasms with which she'd welcomed him into town, between nutty Minerva and the ever-evil Victor, the poor guy hadn't caught a break since he'd allegedly purchased the Gypsy king's box. "Okay. Are you basically telling me that it's been great, but you'll call me?"

He snorted, doing an admirable job of hiding any guilt he might be feeling about leaving her high and dry. This did make her peeved. *The rat bastard.* "I'm telling you it's been great. It'll be greater. Just let me get the damn diary, find the flipping treasure and then we can be back at each other like a pair of frisky monkeys on Spanish fly."

She snickered at the "frisky monkeys" line. "A-a-a-a-aw, shucks, you sweet-talker, you. I'm flattered. Really. But I'll have to pass."

His eyebrows arched and his expression was almost panicked. "What do you mean, you'll have to pass? We're not over yet, Tink. Not by a long shot—"

"I agree."

"Because it's silly to blow off something that might be, well, you know, maybe serious…possibly…"

She snorted. "Hey, you might want to put a few more disclaimers in there. Otherwise, I might get the wrong idea and start catching up on my back issues of *Bride's Magazine*."

He cursed, rubbing his neck. "I'm not saying this right, but when I get back, we'll talk and—"

"Max." She waved her hand in front of his face. "Yoo-hoo. You're not listening. Now pay attention."

"Huh?" His hands had lowered some time ago, and he tossed the box behind him, bouncing it on the far side of the mattress. She'd have dived for it, but he'd have blocked her in a second.

"We'll talk on the way. Because I. Am going. With you. There's nothing you can do to stop me, but I can stop you…."

He crossed his arms over his chest and smirked. "Oh, yeah?"

Fixing him with her best tough-girl leer, she said, "Oh, yeah…. Now strip…."

He started to laugh, but his amusement was quickly choked off with a startled, "Wr-r-r-rg…" His eyes shot wide. His fingers twitched toward the button of his pants, and he froze, then muttered, *"Oh, shit…."*

8

FIFTEEN HOURS LATER, in another country (Russia) in another crappy hotel room (the charming decor more European kitsch, this time, than redneck tacky), and Cassie found herself right smack-dab in the same damn argument with Max Stone.

She was jet-lagged, cranky and not in the mood to get jerked around anymore by the hunky, er, jerk. She'd have thought the infuriating man would've learned his lesson by now, even if he didn't understand the hows and whys of his urge to rip off his clothes and streak every time he'd tried to ditch her. At the airport alone, this had been several times.

He'd finally given up and settled down, and she'd rewarded his good behavior with a temporary ban on all thoughts of the gorgeous freak in his birthday suit. Otherwise, they'd have never been able to board the plane. To punish him, however, they hadn't joined the *mile high club*. No matter how much he'd begged and flattered. He was probably already a charter member, anyway. If all the come-hither glances and never-ending walk-bys from the air stewards—*both* sexes, in case his head wasn't already big enough, and half the passengers—was anything on which to judge his previous travels.

Instead of making whoopee with Max in an under-size lavatory, Cassie had rifled through the overhead compartments for one of those dinky pillows the airlines kept stocked at about three per plane that looked like dry-weave maxi pads without the wings. Then she located a blanket and huffily turned her back on him and tried to catch a few z's. The flirting foot traffic, however, made this impossible.

And now Minerva wasn't answering her phone. A major convenience, but Cassie pretended to be annoyed. And Max was trying to leave her behind for the ump-teenth time. She'd have been madder if he wasn't sporting a boner down his left pant leg practically the size of her forearm. Quite flattering, that.

"You're not going with me to Victor's Midnight Madness sale and that's final," he argued. Again. "It's way too dangerous. I'll be back before you know it."

Cassie flopped onto the bed. They'd already gone round and round on this one. But Cassie's curiosity finally caught up with her and, at the very least, she deserved some answers. "What's the deal with this guy, anyway? And why is he so pissed at you?"

Max rubbed his face, as if he were resigned but realized he owed her an explanation. "There's no short answer on this. He showed up when I was about fifteen, a grad student working for my dad. From the get-go, I knew he was an asshole." He sat down in the vinyl chair facing the bed, settling into his story, fingers lacing together and resting on his stomach.

"Victor would start out nice with people. A total brown-noser. Obviously fake but, right off, most couldn't see it. When a person goes into academics, they don't want to be average, they want to be a genius. An authority in the field. Vic believed that he had all the makings of eventual greatness, but he didn't have the brainpower for that load."

Max stared at some point in the distance, his eyes narrowed. "In a weird way, he was a lot like my dad, only worse. He hated being wrong. Yet he was craftier than my father, more conniving. Knew how to manipulate things so he'd come out looking good. But if someone started to suspect that Vic had more than a bit of hot air blowing, he'd turn on them."

Cassie almost raised her hand and asked if the jerk wad also went by the name of Ron. But she was still confused. Victor sounded like a passive-aggressive pest but not the ultimate villain. Then again, Ron was the antichrist and had left her in need of a psychotherapist. Never mind.

She nodded with sympathy, and said, "Okay, I'm with you. So then what happened?"

Max flashed her a grin and shook his head in amusement. "Vic knew I thought he was an idiot. But he was very clever how he handled my dad. More clever than me," he added, his grin flattening into a smirk. "Back then pretty much anything found at a site belonged to whoever funded the trip. With my dad, this meant the university.

"Anyway, Vic started working the black market—not cataloging everything that had been found—and pieces would go missing. I figured out his game and went to my old man. Vic lied. By this time I was seventeen and looked older. So when Vic claimed it was me, it was somewhat plausible. Said I must've gotten nervous and pointed the finger at him. My dad believed Victor."

At Cassie's outraged gasp, Max laughed. "Thanks, Tink. It wasn't that big of a deal. Turns out Vic did me a favor. I'm the best in the biz. But he's got a weak spot where I'm concerned and he's a jealous prick about my success. I'm sure there's some reason for his craziness but it's like he can't completely buy in to his own delusion as long as I don't." Max shrugged. "So he's always looking to wow me or beat me. One of these days, when he realizes it'll never work, he'll be looking to kill me. But that'll be a while. He's nowhere close yet to giving up our fun and games."

"Kill you?" Okay. That was it. Even someone as awe-inspiring as Max could make the occasional mistake. And Victor sounded even sneakier than Minerva. "Thanks for sharing, but now I'm definitely going with you. You need my help. I'll be your backup."

The rat fink actually expected her to sit in the room and twiddle her thumbs while he willingly walked into a trap. And even more insanely, he refused to leave the box here with her. The idiot might as well gift-wrap the lover's box and slap a big bow on it before he handed it over to Victor. And then she'd *never* get laid again. As if the life-or-death crap wasn't bad enough.

But their basic problem here was trust. Max didn't trust her not to take the box back to Minerva and go after the treasure herself, and she didn't trust him ever to come back and have sex with her once he'd slipped his magical leash, so to speak. After all, the lover's box would be with him. She didn't have a clue how many miles her Gypsy-voodoo sex powers covered. And she wasn't taking any chances.

Max snorted. "Listen, Tink, you're not exactly back-up material."

"Says you. And stop calling me that. I don't look a thing like Tinker Bell."

He grinned, but otherwise ignored her. "Just don't leave the room, and you'll be fine. The last thing Victor would ever imagine is that I'd bring you back with me."

"What, he's seen my picture?" Cassie asked, only half-sarcastically. She wasn't a dog, but she was hardly the type of beauty a guy would drag halfway around the globe because he couldn't bear to let her out of his bed. Let alone a guy as insanely gorgeous as Max. Without the lover's box, he was so far out of her league it was ridiculous.

He rolled his eyes. "Since you can't stop staring at my crotch, you can see that I didn't mean it that way."

She batted her lashes. "I bet you say that to all the girls."

"No, I don't," he said wryly. "Ever."

Boy, was it hot in here, or what? She cleared her throat, then said, "Nice try, slick. You're not distracting me. Now, come on and be reasonable. If you won't let me go with you, then you have to leave the box here."

Max tried to talk over her, but she held up her hand. "Yeah, yeah. You're all that's tough, but what if Mr. Creepy Archenemy has reinforcements? He could have a dozen more of those goons at his beck and call," she said, getting more and more upset. "What if they all try to jump you at once? They might seriously hurt you." Horrified, she added, "Or damage your face."

He coughed into his hand as if he was trying to swallow down a laugh. "Uh, thanks for the concern, but I know what I'm doing. And that's why I'm leaving early. Once I make sure I'm not being followed, I have a few places where I can stash the box. Even if I'm dead, Vic'll never find it."

Cassie shot up from her sprawled position. "Don't say things like that. It's not funny. And what are you implying? That you have hidey-holes in every major city on the planet?"

He gave a casual shrug, the gesture cocky and annoying. "I get around."

"Phuuh," she huffed, then muttered, "I'm sure you do," narrowing her eyes in his direction. Well, she'd put a stop to *that*. And he wasn't taking her box to any *hidey-holes,* either. Cassie's entire sex life was on the line here.

"Look, you can take me with you voluntarily, leave the lover's box here, or…" She let her voice trail off provocatively.

He must have had an inkling of where this was headed, because he started shifting his feet, the movement a wee bit nervous. He was probably telling himself that there was a perfectly logical explanation for his bizarre desire to do the nudey-patooty dance every time he tried to leave her. Well, if Mr. Smarty Pants hadn't figured it out she wasn't about to clue him in.

But Max Stone was made of sterner stuff, and he bravely yet stupidly squared his shoulders and said, "I'm not playing around this time, peanut. I'll…uh… I'll…" his gaze darted around the room as if searching for inspiration. "I'll tie you to the bed if I have to," he finished triumphantly.

While her heart jolted as if he'd uttered the password to some secret door buried deep in her psyche, he strode over to the gym bag that he'd earlier retrieved at one of their stops at a back alley shop once they'd arrived in St. Petersburg. She still couldn't figure out what the store actually sold, and Max wouldn't tell her.

Before she could blink, however, Max opened the zipper and took out a folding knife that looked fairly wicked when he flipped it open.

Cassie yelped. "Whoa, look at the size of that puppy. So-o-o-o, what are you going to do with that bad boy?" She knew he wouldn't hurt her, but she was off the bed in a shot. Momentarily distracted from operation Get Max Starkers Then Bend Him To Her Licentious Will, her jaw dropped open and she gaped like a rube idiot.

"Make a gag for you," he said dryly, teasing her. At least she hoped he was teasing. "What do you think I'm doing? You won't listen, and I don't trust you not to follow after me. I'm tying you to the bed." Then, with all the flair of a magician whipping a tablecloth from beneath a full set of dishes, he jerked the top sheet off the bed and snapped it in the air.

"Show-off." Why wasn't she pissed? Getting tied up and waiting a few hours like a prisoner was *not* part of the plan. Maybe the other way around. But not with her spread-eagled for his delectation. And why was she getting suspiciously wet south of the border? *Uh-oh...*

"Thank you. Now quit yapping and lie down."

"*Shyeah*, right. In your dreams." Or hers. Cassie absently fanned her face, her gaze darting around for a thermostat. Surely somebody had cranked up the heat.

Meanwhile, he'd made four cuts at one end of the fabric. He pocketed the knife, snared her gaze, then dramatically ripped the sheet down the center. Cassie almost swooned.

While she stood there, watching and panting like a total slut puppy, he walked over to the bed. The headboard was nailed to the wall. She stared mesmerized while he anchored his makeshift bondage aids to the metal bed frame, letting the free ends drape onto the mattress from each corner. They were seductive and threatening. Max gave a wicked chuckle.

This was bad. Very, very bad...

Snap out of it, she desperately scolded her newfound inner submissive. She'd finally started down the road to badassness, and this was in no way the time to wimp out. If she was playing bind-and-spank-the-naughty-sex-slave then she had to be the master.

Youch—just the thought of playing dom to Max's sub made her nipple ring zap and throb like a divining rod. Okay, apparently she was a little kinky. Because this new twist got her even more hot and bothered than she'd been a minute ago.

She rubbed her breast, her nipple stinging deliciously, and Max suddenly stood bolt-straight and his own hand flew to his hip and he hissed out a breath.

Max's eyes shot so wide she could see the whites around his irises as he froze. "I don't know how you're doing that, but quit it."

Good. It was time to wrangle back control, and she swallowed and said, "Uh-h-h…" *Whoops. That couldn't be right.* She coughed and tried again.

"Well, I guess by now you know the drill." Hey, at least her voice didn't squeak. She gestured toward his khaki-colored ensemble. "It's gettin' hot in here, so why don't you take off all your clothes."

Standing still as a statue, Max gaped at her. Finally, he cleared his throat, and said, "Cassie, I have no idea what you're up to, but stop messing around."

But it was as if he couldn't help himself now that he'd given in and moved, and he reached back and grabbed the neck of his T-shirt. Then he tugged it forward over his head in that special way that guys took off their shirts. Cassie had always found this maneuver quite yummy and her stomach gave a slow flip.

"Fine," he managed to say, sounding as if it had been an effort to find his voice. "We'll do it once before I leave, but then I'm getting the diary by myself."

She *tsked* and shook her head. "Max, Max…I don't think you should have said that."

The sheer beauty of him still took her breath away, and, as stunning as his perfectly toned torso was, bruises and all, she was flooded with the overwhelming desire to see the rest of him…. Now.

As if compelled by forces beyond his control, his mouth worked soundlessly and his face filled with panic. Immediately, he ripped free the laces on his boots, toed them off, then tore open the button at his fly and shucked his pants. Of course, Max went commando.

There were only two words to describe the privilege of seeing Max Stone in the buff: shock and awe.

"Before you start bossing me around…" he croaked "…and I completely lose it, I have a request."

Cassie cocked an eyebrow. She was digging her new dom vibe and wasn't sure she was in the mood for requests. But she was interested to hear what he wanted, and said, "Fine. Request away."

"This time I want to do it normal." There was a slight tremor buzzing through his frame and his erection was as hard and huge as she'd ever seen it. He was definitely riding the edge here. "I mean intercourse," he rushed on to clarify. "Regular intercourse. Nothing fancy. No tricks. Just you and me. And I'm on top."

Cassie popped the button on her jeans and lowered the zipper. The rasp of the metal teeth clicking open was strangely erotic. "Hmm. To me, that sounded more like a command than a request." She used her heel to slip out of first one sneaker then the next. Then she took off her socks. Her jeans and her shirt she left on for now.

She turned away from him, shaking out her hair, then walked to the foot of the bed. Beneath her top, her nipple ring was doing its thing and heat washed through her breast, immediately sparking an answering pulse between her legs.

Behind her, she heard Max start twice before he managed to say, "Yeah, well, for now, those are my rules. Otherwise, I'm not doing it." She cast a quick glance back over her shoulder.

"You think so…?"

As he stood there, every muscle in his body appeared to be contracted, like a body builder at a competition except without the funny poses. And his hands kept opening, then closing into fists at his side. The man was fighting it as hard as he could. And Cassie knew exactly who was going to win.

"Yes." His voice actually cracked, and he coughed. "Wait a minute. What were we talking about?"

Standing at the end of the bed, she slowly, oh, so slowly slipped her shirt upward, then pulled it over her head. "You were saying that you would only have sex with me if we did it your way. You on top."

"Yeah. That's right. That's, uh…" his words trailed off as she moved her hands up to her breasts, softly cupping her own weight, then gently using her fingers to stimulate her nipples. She let her head fall back and closed her eyes.

Since Max was behind her, she knew that from his view the knowledge of what she was obviously doing would be more arousing than if he'd been sitting front row center. He let out a hiss of breath as he cursed long and low.

"Just get on the bed, Cassie. On your back. Now."

"Soon," she crooned, enjoying every luscious second of her own touch when she never had in this way before. Picturing herself exactly as he'd see her, she skimmed her palms down from her breasts, over her stomach then inside the front of her pants, exaggerating each move of her arms, arching her back, lifting her bottom toward him as her fingers slipped between her curls.

She let the pad of her middle finger caress the raised pearl of sensation in her moist heat. She groaned, her hair sliding against her back.

"Sweet hell," Max said on a rush of air. But she wasn't done pushing him, and she lowered her jeans from her hips down to puddle at her ankles. She stepped out of them, then widened her legs and bent forward. Then she went back to touching and rubbing, stroking and playing with the wet heat at the apex of her thighs, knowing that Max could see every delicious flick and swirl she gifted herself.

He choked out a primal growl and the hairs at the back of her neck lifted, chills rushing across her skin. Oh, she'd pushed him all right, possibly further than even she could handle with her new persona. She could feel silken moisture leak from her core in delicious throbs while her nipples pulled painfully tight, contracted to tiny rocks of flesh, hard and burning for his tongue and mouth.

If this didn't happen soon her heart would be permanently injured from banging against her ribs. "You want to be on top, right, Max?" she asked, climbing onto the bed, then crawling on her hands and knees in the most graphic way possible.

"Yes." He said just the one word, his voice a grumble that skittered straight up her spine.

When she reached the headboard, she took hold of the strips of sheet that he'd earlier tied to the frame. Holding each one in her fist, she then circled her wrists, winding the slack around and around until the strips became more like tethered handles than bindings. Her arms were splayed, but she still had some give, resting on her elbows so her breasts swayed and brushed on the linens beneath her.

She widened her knees, arched her back, then glanced over her shoulder at Max and finished what she knew would be an invitation he couldn't refuse. "Then what are you waiting for? Climb on…."

MAX WAS AFRAID TO EVEN BLINK. He tried to swallow, his throat catching around the lump of heat that had swelled behind his Adam's apple. *Oh, shit. Oh, shit….*

This is not what he'd meant, and the tiny goddess was playing him for all she was worth, which happened to be a hell of a fucking lot. She was hot and juicy and sweet. So flipping sweet. She'd be like warm syrup on his tongue and his mouth went from parched to watering as he climbed onto the bed, prowling up behind her. She wriggled her world-class tush, rocking back toward him, taunting and begging.

His hands shook as they clamped on to her curves. Hard. Almost a smack, which she deserved. And Cassie, the finest piece of tail he'd ever encountered, actually purred. His heart started pounding and he had no doubt that his blood pressure had shot high enough to give him a stroke.

He squeezed his fingers tight into her lush softness, holding her still. "Don't move," he rasped, though why he bothered was a mystery, since she *never* listened to him. But she was going to this time and he tightened his hold and lowered his mouth to the satiny skin at the small of her back. He licked and kissed, using his lips, his tongue, his teeth. She was soft, softer than anything he'd ever felt and she smelled like honey. She groaned, her upper body swaying since he'd frozen her pelvis to his will.

He slid down and dropped to his elbows then rotated his hold and anchored her in place with his forearms against her inner thighs and his palms cupped around the front of her hips. He had all the leverage and he pulled her spread bounty to his waiting mouth. Her back arched deeper.

He kissed her like he was kissing her mouth, and at the first flick of his tongue against her folds, she cried out and his ears just kept on ringing. He loved this, absolutely loved it—everything about it—and could have licked and eaten her glistening sweetness for days. Any chance he got, he'd be back down between her legs worshipping her the way he craved.

She pushed against his face and he groaned and lost himself, gently devouring her.

The skin on his cock ached, stretched harder than he could ever remember, and he thrust himself against the bed, desperate to be inside her but not wanting to miss a second of what he was doing now.

And she made it so easy for him, gasping and squealing whenever he gave her a particularly inventive swirl or stroke. But her favorite, the one that made her back go loose then made her stiffen up and her flesh quiver against his open mouth, was a wide flat lick. Over and over, right from the stiff hood at the *V* of her inner lips to her juicy core. Over and over, lapping at her, slow and steady. No rush, nowhere to go, anything and everything to make her scream and come on his face. So he could breathe her in and be part of her, touch her heart and her soul over and over again. So she'd never leave him and he'd never be alone, or know a day without her.

Nothing was as good as being with her, loving her, touching her. He could not lose this, could never get enough.

Oh, shit. This, this *feeling* wasn't what he'd planned, either, but he didn't care.

He puckered his slippery lips around the stiff hood of her clitoris, then gently sucked her with steady yet strong pulls, and she came apart all over him, rubbing and sliding against his mouth and chin while her legs collapsed in his hold.

He quieted her, nice and slow, soothing yet erotic for long, long seconds while she came down. Meanwhile, he felt like he had a club between his legs and he had to get inside her now. Right now. While she was wide open and totally his. Nothing hidden. Nothing held back.

Somehow she'd broken through all his barriers, every one. Stripped him of more than his clothes—down to the element of who he was, who he wanted to be…with her….

He wiped his mouth on his shoulder, twisting his head, then climbed over her. He hung there, on his hands and knees, panting, staring down at her. *Oh, man.* He was so screwed. Twisting in the wind. Tied in knots. Flat-out gone over her.

Her beautiful face was turned to the side, her mouth open while a tear leaked from her closed eyes. He watched one silvery drop slip down her cheek, and something twisted and burned deep in his chest.

"You're amazing," he whispered, lowering his lips to her temple. "Absolutely amazing. I don't think I'll ever be able to get enough of you." He was dazed and rambling, speaking his thoughts aloud.

"Oh, Max." She smiled so sweetly, a special smile that he somehow knew she'd never given to anyone but him. Wires were firing inside his head, circuits blowing.

He nuzzled her cheek, the corner of her mouth, ran his nose along hers while the weight of his engorged shaft dropped the head of his cock to slide down the crease of her bottom.

As worn out as she was, she moaned, "Please, please be inside me. All of you."

He lowered his hips to the back of hers, her curves warm and lush beneath him. She was so wet and open, the tip of his length inherently found its target and he started pressing forward. He pushed, not rocking, but slow and steady pressure that gave way beneath him.

She sucked in her breath, and he hesitated, but she whispered, "Don't stop. Keep going," and he did.

His mouth couldn't leave her skin, and he rained kisses across the side of her face, over her jaw, behind her ear and down her neck. Her back was cushioned to his chest, and he reached forward and grabbed the two strips of sheet that she was holding on to for dear life, placing his palms above hers.

Caging her in with his entire body, steadily penetrating her from behind, he felt huge, everywhere. She was so much smaller, so vulnerable, and it brought every protective instinct he'd never even known he possessed roaring to life. She shivered beneath him as he finally, finally slid all the way inside her, the muscles in his arms flexing as he used the ties to sling himself that last, luscious bit deeper.

Mindlessly, she whispered his name over and over, begging and asking him for things she probably wasn't even aware of. He pressed his face to her neck, and she arched her head back against his shoulder.

He was afraid to move, her tight heat excruciating as her inner muscles clamped around his shaft. And then reality hit him right in the nads.

"Oh, crap. I don't have a condom on."

Max hadn't gone free willy since he was a teenager. Never. And while he was strict on this rule, he wanted to whimper at the thought of pulling out of her and rolling on a rubber.

Somehow she managed to get out the fairly lengthy explanation between gasps and pants, "I'm on the pill. Started taking it when I was engaged. But Ron broke up with me before I'd been on it for a month. I've never done it without a condom."

This was the first Max had heard of any fiancé, and he did not like the reaction it set off inside him. Not one little bit. But warring with the rush of sheer possessive jealousy was the realization that neither one of them had had unprotected sex in the past decade, and that he was getting the go-ahead in a very major way.

"Me, neither. Crap." He shook his head. "I mean, I'm safe. This is a first for me, too, baby. Are you okay with this? Skin to skin. You and me. I'd never put you at risk. I'll always keep you safe." And he meant it. Every single blessed word.

"Yes, yes," she mumbled in that breathy, on-the-verge-of-coming way that she had, and he felt his balls tighten.

He let go of the strips of sheet to run his hand along the sides of her chest, caressing and stroking as he set up the barest of paces with his hips. He was not going to last here. No way. And he wanted her with him every step of the way because he didn't want her left behind when he lost control.

He was whispering things in her ear, things he didn't even want to hear himself, but he meant them. What he was going to do to her and how she made him feel. And then she was pushing back against him, or trying to, anyway, because she didn't have the right angle to get the pressure she needed.

He slid his hands beneath hers, spreading them wide and she frantically twisted her own free of the strips of cloth that she'd been gripping. She clamped hold of his forearms, using his limbs to push her pelvis back into his.

He kept pressing into her, barely thrusting, more shoving as deep as he could get while she circled and shoved back. But before long, the greedy little goddess wanted more and he started moving his hips, back and forth. And then she flat-out went wild beneath him.

She was getting hard to hold on to, and he moved one arm underneath her, between her breasts, his hand gripped to her shoulder so he wouldn't screw her right up the headboard and out from under him.

Her tits bounced against his arm with each plunge, while inside her slick heat was a constant squeezing pleasure. Her inner walls rippled and contracted and pressure swelled down low in his body. He hunched over her, going faster and harder, working himself in and out, over and over. Things were giving way inside his head, his body outside his control.

Victor and a hundred thugs could have broken in the hotel room door and nothing would have stopped him. Max wasn't just having sex. Hell, they'd even moved beyond making love. He was marking her as his, and it still wasn't enough.

"Are you ready? Come on, Cassie…." He wasn't coming without her. His body was losing its rhythm, and it took every bit of his concentration to hold on. She finally cried out, then clamped down so tightly around him it almost hurt.

The first contraction of her release made the corners of his vision dim. He squeezed his eyes closed and his jaw clenched on a yell ripped from the center of his chest. Lightning heat raced up his groin, then exploded, his cock jerking violently with each dramatic beat of orgasm.

He didn't know how much time had passed before he was back, aware of his surroundings, and he wrapped his arm around her waist, then lowered them both to their sides, spooning her to his chest, their bodies still deeply linked while he fought to breathe.

He buried his face in her hair. She smelled like him. He'd marked her all over, and it felt good and right. Like he could let out a sigh of relief. Then Max had a thought, and grinned. *Okay.* Technically she'd let him be on top. But he didn't care what kind of tricks she tried to pull, he still wasn't letting her get anywhere near Victor….

9

AN HOUR OR SO LATER, Max and Cassie sat in the plain, compact car he'd borrowed from one of his local friends, casing the swank house Victor was renting.

The International Antiquities League conference was going on and Victor had appearances to keep. There was no way his university would cover the splashy crib, so it was obviously his smuggling sideline that was footing the bill.

So far, Max had spotted two men patrolling the perimeter and one through the upstairs window. He recognized them and knew there was one more missing.

Victor was such an amoral jerk-off he had to travel around like a gangster rapper with his posse. The university board believed his retinue was the result of kidnapping threats over some inherited riches. There was no inheritance—he was pretty sure Vic had been spawned, not birthed—and the only threats were for death, not kidnapping. Max had made most of them himself, although there were certainly others waiting in the wings.

Victor had aspirations far beyond his scope. And when little men were pushed too far against the wall, they could become trouble. Victor might as well have Napoleon Complex engraved on his forehead. With Cassie around, this went from an annoyance to a worry.

But the sale wasn't for another couple of hours, and Max already knew what he was going to do.

Unfortunately, he had no control over the goddess and he was tired of fighting her. Besides, he lost every time and it was getting embarrassing. Though she was definitely staying in the car. He'd go inside bare-ass naked if he had to.

How the hell did she *do* that? Tired of racking his brain for a logical explanation, other than sheer animal lust or another four-letter *L* word, he ignored the conundrum.

Cassie happily popped another French fry into her mouth, and started munching. Max took a sip of his soda, wishing they served vodka, supersized, at the local fast food drive-through where they'd stopped on the way here. He sure as hell needed one.

He sighed, then finished off his burger, chewing sullenly. Fine. He was pouting. But he refused to admit why.

Finally he couldn't take it another second, and he said darkly, "So, tell me about this fiancé of yours."

She wrinkled her nose. "He's not my fiancé anymore. We broke up. Or, rather, he dumped me." She waved her fry for emphasis.

Max snorted. "Idiot."

"Yep." She nodded. "That's what I think."

"Did you love him?"

Apparently Max had gone ahead and given himself over to the dark side, voluntarily pursuing topics with a female that he'd never before in his life ever entertained. It wasn't a conscious decision; he just couldn't seem to stop his flapping lips. Next he'd be asking her about her feelings and listening to light rock on the radio.

Cassie shot him a quick look, her expression somewhat surprised. Hell, apparently even she knew that a guy like him did not initiate the ex-lover conversation unless he was being held at gunpoint. Then she shrugged. "I must have thought so at some point, but in hindsight he was a putz."

Fine. He was not going to chase after more info. Usually women were anxious to give a running bio on every male they'd ever dragged into their beds, then analyze the wheres and whys of what went wrong. But not Cassie. Of course not. The one time he wanted a woman to spill her guts, she was being discreet.

"Why'd he break up with you?" Well, the shocks just kept coming, and he was a horse's ass. But he couldn't imagine why some jerk-off would dump her.

Also, if she had any secret annoying habits, other than busting his chops, being a smart-ass and turning his hair gray, it was best that he find out now. Or that's what he told himself, not ready to admit that he'd become a total loser.

Cassie sighed. "I don't suppose you'd be satisfied if I said that he just wasn't that into me?"

Max smirked, and she groused, "Fine, fine. Let's

see. Well, since Ron's a liar, his excuses are suspect, but he said that I wouldn't make a good wife because I didn't respect his authority in our relationship."

Well! The man had probably been on to something there, but that was half of the pixie goddess's charm. She was feisty as hell. Then Max winced, realizing that all his ordering and bossing her around must have gone over like the proverbial lead balloon. No wonder she did the opposite of whatever he said.

"Um, also he never seemed interested in sex, thought I was too fat and, by the end, pretty much ragged on everything I did. Obviously, he wasn't such a creep in the beginning, but as time went on he got more and more controlling. He was good at it. Very subtle. He'd criticize me in a hundred different ways, then somehow make it look like he was the injured party, and that it had been either speak out for both our sakes, or live in misery. Personally, I think he's the Antichrist and will be responsible for wheeling in Armageddon, but I could be wrong."

"Whoa." Max blew out a breath, not knowing where to attack that onslaught of crap. "Well, I can't picture anyone getting away with giving you orders, and the rest is bullshit. Though, I'm sure you're right on the apocalypse thing."

Feeling much better about the fiancé, he tapped softly on the steering wheel. He didn't even care that he'd been jealous, something that should have him freaking right the hell out. She hated her ex, and, for the moment, that was enough.

He tried to turn his thoughts back to the treasure, but

noticed that Cassie had gotten quiet. He frowned. "You know he was full of it, right? You don't believe any of that garbage, do you?"

"Well, I'm not a complete waste of space, but I have my flaws. One of them, undeniably, being my fat butt," she muttered.

Max scowled and jerked his gaze to hers. "You're kidding, right?"

"About my butt being fat?" Her eyebrows flew up her forehead. "Well, no. Not really."

"You have to know that you're incredibly sexy. Just the thought of your backside is enough to make my palms sweat. My vote is that the ex is gay."

Cassie waved off his slavish adoration. At least, that's how it seemed to him.

"You can't help that," she said offhandedly, giving a shrug. "You just think you like my derriere. Normally, you wouldn't. But that's okay."

Max did a double take, shooting her a look that he hoped conveyed his Alice-falling-down-the-flippin'-bunghole sensation. "When you speak, do the words make any sense to you? Seriously. Because I don't think they could."

"Anyway," she cut in loudly, "enough about my butt." Then she quickly, and not so subtly, changed the topic. "So what's your plan to get back our diary?"

He noticed that it was *your* plan, but *our* diary. For some reason this didn't bother him like it normally did. He was especially starting to like the *our* part. *Hell*.

Rather than address his latest personal revelation, he

decided to go along with Cassie's attempt to change the subject. "Well, first I make sure that an eager buyer doesn't try to show up early. That would mean that somebody had made Victor an offer he felt was a better risk than the possibility of finding the treasure. I already know two of the guys who are coming. I'm better than they are, so they don't worry me. But I couldn't find out anything about the third one, and that does."

"*How* do you know these things?" she demanded.

"I have been doing this for a while. I put money in the right hands and I learn things. Or somebody owes me a favor, and so on." He grinned at her shocked look. "How did you think it worked? Crystal ball?"

She sniffed. "Never mind. You were saying?" she prompted.

"If the third buyer hasn't shown up by thirty minutes before showtime, then he's coming on time and is probably just a regular player. You stay in the car and keep a lookout from under a blanket in the backseat. I mean it." Before she could interrupt, he added, "Yes, yes, with the lover's box. Then I create a diversion. While Victor and his muscle are distracted, I break in, steal the diary, and we split."

"Seriously. What's your plan? Because that's like the worst one I've ever heard."

"Heard a lot of 'em, have you?"

"Fine. Whatever. No doubt the diary will just be sitting out waiting for you after you throw a few fire-crackers into the backyard."

"No. Victor will put the diary inside the wall safe that

comes with the rental. I've already scoped out the security. I know how to bypass the system, and Victor always uses the same combination. He's dumb that way."

The goddess blinked. Then she shrugged and loudly vacuumed up the final dregs of her jumbo diet soda with her straw. She was going to regret that when she was dying to pee and had to stay in the car or hit the bushes.

"Fine," she said. "What about weapons? I saw your knife, so you're packing steel. What about heat? I'm sure you'll need firepower. If one of those guys tries to lay a hand on you, I want you to shoot or stab first, and ask questions later."

Max tried not to gawk. His pixie had turned bloodthirsty and was starting to sound like a badly written cop show.

"And you should probably leave something with me if you have extra—"

"Not a chance in hell! Jeez, Tink. You're small, but vicious. Remind me not to cross you. Ever."

"The goons already tried to beat you up once when they broke into Minerva's shop, and this Victor is a jerk and always bothering you. It's been two days and I'm already sick of it."

Max rubbed his nose, hiding a grin. "Thanks, but I don't need a mommy. Especially one who wants me to annihilate anyone who crosses my path."

She laughed, then tentatively reached across the seat and took his hand, her fingers slipping between his. Shockingly, it was as intimate as anything they'd done sexually. Her mouth was curved in that special smile he was sure she reserved just for him, and he swore something shifted behind his sternum. She also had a hard gleam in her eye.

Somehow, he'd fallen into her protective circle, and heaven help the poor sap who tried to harm him. He could honestly say that he'd never encountered the like before. No one had cared about him. Maybe his mother, before she'd died, but that was so long ago he couldn't remember.

Max's chest pulled tight, and it hurt to breathe. And it was time for him to jump out of the car and create his diversion.

Damn. He did not want to leave her. For the first time in his life fear, real and palpable, swelled through his gut. The stakes mattered this time. After his father had kicked him out, Max had shut off his feelings and he feared that this woman had turned them back on full blast.

"Hey, Stone, you okay?" Cassie tilted her head.

He gently took hold of her face, their coupled hands curled against one of her cheeks, and his fingers spread to caress the other. He lowered his mouth to hers, licking his tongue between her lips, sliding deep into her mouth as if he were sipping something he couldn't live without. And damn if this wasn't the truth.

He'd never felt this before, and already it hurt. She was too important. Vital at some core level. He wanted to forget about the damn treasure and get her the hell out of here.

The thought made him stiffen, and he slowly pulled away. He looked down into her pretty face, her eyes loopy just from kissing him. There was something about her that grabbed him and didn't let go. Not once since he'd met her had he stopped feeling the pull. That had never happened to him before. What the hell was she doing to him?

Before he could stop himself, he said, "Do. Not. Leave. The. Car. If I'm not back in ten minutes, drive off without me. Go straight to Minerva. I'll find you."

Then he opened the door and got out, before he changed his mind.

NINE MINUTES LATER, Max came around the back corner of the house in a flat run, the car in his sights. The plan Cassie had mocked had gone like clockwork, and he almost laughed in victory. Screwing Victor was too damn easy.

Then, from the corner of his eye, he spotted the goddess hunched over a black lump in the grass, swinging a massive branch like it was a bat.

"Cassie!" he hissed. "What the holy hell are you doing?"

She let out a startled yip and dropped her weapon of mass destruction. "I don't know who he is, but he was going to hurt you," she babbled, her words gushing out in rush. "See? He had a gun. I knocked it from his hand." She practically danced on her toes, pointing to the Glock now gleaming darkly on the grass.

Max glanced back over his shoulder. Victor hadn't sounded the alarm yet but that could change at any second. The guy on the ground wasn't one of Victor's men.

"I told you to stay in the car," he growled. *Dammit.* She was not to be left alone. His violent little menace would knock the lights out of anyone who threatened him. "How do you know he was going to hurt me?"

"Please. Like he was taking his gun for a nighttime walk."

Okay, so her victim was definitely dangerous, but this only made what she'd done worse. Did she not have a single ounce of self-preservation? She was absolutely fearless. And it was totally ridiculous. If she didn't get herself killed, he'd do the honors himself just to get it over with. The suspense was making him demented.

He rolled the man to his side. The moonlight hit his face and Max immediately recognized the FSS officer. And not just any old FSS officer, either. Muttering a string of the most obscene curses he could think of, he felt for a pulse, found one, then grabbed Cassie's arm in a viselike hold and hauled her toward the car.

"Get in, get in," he urged. He shoved her into her seat, then got behind the wheel, and had the engine running before the door slammed shut after him. Smoke poured from the back tires as he popped the clutch, then they took off into the street, the engine screaming.

Hell, hell, hell. Max's heart was pounding so hard he could hear his pulse swooshing past his eardrums. *The FSS! What a cluster fu—*

"So, who was that guy? Did you know him?"

"Buckle your seat belt," Max barked at her. He chewed his bottom lip. What the frick was the spookiest spook in the Russian ranks, Ivan Petrutrio, doing at Victor's? And how the hell had Cassie gotten the jump on him? The goddess had managed to do what a trained cadre of international spies wouldn't attempt.

"Gripe, gripe, nag, nag," she complained, oblivious to how close she'd come to, at the very least, a long stay in one of the underground rooms beneath the offices of the former KGB, and at most—dead. Innocent people checked in, but they didn't check out.

The FSS stood for the Federal Service of Security. It served the same scary-ass function as the KGB, just under a new name. But it was even more lethal and ruthless. Russia's answer to democracy was not working and the country had pretty much returned to its old ways.

Picture every movie where members of the KGB were portrayed as the villains, then double their brutal menace, and you had the new FSS. Except the FSS didn't get written about in the press like the KGB of the eighties because the Middle East kept hogging the limelight. Oh, and the FSS killed off any reporters stupid enough to try and expose it. There was no screwing around with this new incarnation of the old evil.

"Yeesh. What's got *you* so worked up? I took care of that guy and we're both alive and breathing."

"For the moment. And you have no idea what you've just done."

Frankly, Max wasn't too sure, either. The FSS was not only rife with killers but crooks, as well. They were known to accept bribes from thieves, smugglers and other friends of the black market. For the right price, the FSS didn't care what went in or out of their borders as long as it wasn't something it wanted for the mother country. Max regularly dealt with guys way lower down the food chain than Ivan Petrutrio. But *after* he'd found a relic. The FSS wasn't interested in the legwork, just the euros he gave agents to look the other way.

Max knew the score, and always factored in a certain percentage for bribes. But Ivan Petrutrio was too high up to get involved with a piddly diary written by a dead Gypsy's lover unless something major was going down. Even if the FSS believed the treasure was real, they wouldn't be interested unless the total haul was worth millions and millions. Ivan Petrutrio could get a reasonable stash of jewels anytime he wanted. There was nothing in the legend to suggest the treasure was greater than what he could extort from the Russian Mafia with a snap of his fingers.

Besides, politics was Ivan's game. He made men disappear. Permanently. Whatever his reason for being at Victor's, it meant hugely bad news for Max and Cassie….

"What? Didn't your plan work?" she teased. "I told you, you needed to think that one out better—"

"I got the diary," he spoke over her, breaking in before her next smart-mouthed crack. The vein in his temple was pounding hard enough to burst. "Forget about that. Did you bring your passport with you? It's not back at the room, is it?"

She hesitated, then reached down and patted her backpack. "I have it."

"Good." That meant he could keep driving, and get them as far away as possible from the gangbang waiting to break loose back there. "Now. I want to hear exactly what happened. You are going to start with, 'I saw a bad guy lurking in the shadows,' and finish with, 'then I brained him with a giant stick.'"

"Hey, boss me around, why don't ya?" she said, then must have realized that she'd pushed him too far, because she quickly complied. "Fine, fine, I was waiting in the car like you told me, but, pretty much right after you left, I really, really, er, had to *go*. Damn supersized drink—"

The corner of Max's eye started twitching. *Cripes.* She was giving him a nervous tic. But he'd known that damn drink was going to be a problem. It was like taking care of a frigging toddler.

"So, I scooted over to the bushes, and before I could get back in the car, I had this intuition that someone was creeping around. Like my spidey-senses were buzzing. I kept my eyes peeled, and saw the sneak slipping along the fence like a shadow. Well, that was enough for me. I knew that any second you were going to come hotfooting it for the car, and I couldn't just let you meet him head-on. What if he'd had a gun? Which he did," she added smugly.

"But I didn't know that, yet. So I started looking around for something to hit him with, just in case. By the way, whoever maintains the lawn at Victor's place sucks, because there were branches everywhere."

"Peanut…focus," he growled warningly.

"I am. Yeesh. Anyway, I spotted a nice thick one—

light enough for me to pick up, but not too long for me to swing if I needed to clobber him quick—and headed his way."

Max groaned. Or maybe whimpered was more accurate.

"And let me tell ya, he scared the life out of me. 'Cause he turned real quick, and I could see him pull something big and black from inside his coat as he came around. But Mr. Sneaky moved too fast, and tripped over something in the yard. Well, the rat bastard went down. I lowered the boom on his wrist, knocked the gun away and gave him another hit on his thick skull before he could grab for it and start shooting. Then you showed up."

"Unbelievable…." What was the saying about God protecting fools and drunkards?

The fool riding shotgun asked, "Are you sure you're okay? You keep acting all jumpy. It's not like you."

"I've been jumpy since I met you. You're bad for me that way."

"Oh, cut it out. But, hey, now I see why you do it." She beamed over at him, her eyes shining in the dash lights, full of the pounding thrill of excitement.

Max frowned. "Do what?" He downshifted around a turn. He really needed to pull over and figure out where they were going. And have a huge drink. And tie the goddess up and stash her somewhere safe.

"Live like you do. You know, hunt relics. Follow the chase wherever it leads you. Fight the bad guys." She stopped and snickered. "Well. Not that you're a *good* guy, exactly."

Max scowled harder while Cassie kept blathering.

"But you know what I mean. Why you court danger. Pit your wits against the other hunters. Live for the thrill."

"Is that how you see me?" He glared over at her. "Some selfish thrill junky who cares only about when he can get the next rush?"

Cassie grinned. "Well, no. You do it for the money, too. But, hey, don't get me wrong. I can be as shallow as the next gal."

Max opened his mouth to blast her, then stopped. Okay, so she had him pegged. But that was before he'd met her, and it had been fine for him, not for her. Of course, he wasn't finding anything about his current hunt fun or exciting anymore. Other than the sex. And they didn't need to go after the treasure to do that.

Hell, no jewels were worth going up against the FSS with Cassie along for the ride. Max did not want her on Ivan's radar. Period. Victor and his vendetta against Max and everything he touched was bad enough.

Chuckling as if she'd proven her point and they were both on the same daredevil team, she crossed her arms over her chest and leaned back in her seat, closing her eyes.

Hopefully she'd chattered herself out, and he'd have a moment's peace just to think. Nothing made sense, dammit. Was Ivan the third buyer? Or had he gotten some kind of tip? Surely Victor wasn't dumb enough to have approached him on his own. Guys like Ivan silenced people. Forever.

The only other option, the one that made a knot of

fear coil in his gut, was that the government was interested for other reasons.

As he'd said, Russia was falling into its old ways. Journalists conveniently committing suicide if they spoke against the parties in power. An assassination in a friendly suburb of Washington, D.C., when an ex-agent started talking too much about the new regime. If the motherland was flexing its muscle, then something big was going down…. Or something big already had and they were covering their tracks…and Max was taking early retirement.

Maybe it really was time for a new job. Max had socked away more than enough money to quit now if he wanted. *Hell*. It wasn't like he played the black market because he had some deep-seated need to prove his father wrong. Or right, that is. Like he gave a crap that his old man had been a jealous asshole because, even as teenager, Max was better than him at finding artifacts.

So his dad was selfish and had jumped on the chance to believe Victor over his own son. Max didn't give a shit. He'd lived his life exactly how he'd wanted, and damned the consequences…. Suddenly, however, all he wanted was Cassie, a boring life in suburbia—preferably a gated community—and nothing more exciting than crabgrass in his cookie-cutter lawn. Anything to keep her safe and out of trouble.

Speaking of miniterminator, the goddess stretched in her seat and did that hip-wiggle, hair-toss thing that always shot him rock hard. "Hey," she said, her voice going all soft and sexy, "why don't we really try living dangerously. How about a quickie in the car?"

If he didn't have to grip the steering wheel just to keep his hands from shaking, he might have been tempted. It annoyed him to see her so relaxed, though, when he so wasn't, and he said, "Oh, you like living the dangerous life, all right. You just tagged a high-ranking officer of the FSS back there."

She stilled her sexy squirming. "What are you talking about? What's the FSS?"

Max smirked. "Russia's not-so-politically-correct answer to the KGB. New name, same job description. Except scarier and they answer to fewer people."

"KGB? That man I clobbered with a stick?"

"FSS."

"Huh." She didn't look scared at all. "Well," she sniffed, "he shouldn't have been skulking around in the dark."

"That's what spies do."

"Whatever. You're safe. That's all that matters."

Had aliens abducted her brain? He didn't need a woman a foot shorter and at least fifty pounds lighter than him running interference. Lord. It was sweet as hell and made his heart beat in a funky rhythm, but she was going to put him in the loony bin if she didn't cut it out.

"Okay, forget a quickie," she merrily jabbered on. "How about a slowie? Now that we've got Stasi's diary and Rajko's box, let's hit our hotel, have some wild pagan sex, then go find the treasure after we catch a few winks."

He had to hand it to her, his goddess might be a total whack job, but she was a sex machine.

"Hey, didn't we pass the road to our hotel?"

"Yes. A while ago. But until I find out why the big boys of the FSS are interested in Stasi's diary, I don't think it's a good idea to go back there. It was terrifying enough when I only had to worry about you tangling with Victor. You'd get hurt, but you'd still be around. Ivan Petrutrio plays on a whole different level."

She frowned, her sudden concern palpable. Knowing Cassie, however, she was worried for him not herself. *Damn.* Being on the receiving end of unconditional adoration was not as heart-warming as it seemed. His ticker was going to give out before he even got a chance at the warm fuzzies stage.

"So, why would the Russian government care about Stasi's diary?"

Max sighed and rubbed the back of his neck. "That's the question, Tink. That's the question…."

"What if the guy I clobbered was your third buyer?"

"Then we're dealing with something way bigger than I thought… And I have no idea what that could be."

She made a humming noise, then eventually said, "Too bad with all your connections you don't know any Gypsies we could bunk down with. While you tried to figure out what the big bad FSS wants with Stasi's diary, we could stay under their radar, and see if the area Romanis have any stories on Rajko or his lover that you haven't already heard."

Max hit his mental breaks. "What did you say?"

"Well, the Gypsies hid Stasi from her jerky husband. Or whatever your father's theory was. I was just making a joke. You know, ha-ha. Too bad we can't hide out with them until the FSS angle is tromped, and pick their brains for other legends about Rajko and Stasi. I don't know, maybe get our fortunes told, learn a few steps of those lusty dances they're known for." She smiled, her thoughts starting to veer toward la-la land. "I can see you now in tight black pants, a blousy shirt—white, maybe red—the guitars strumming as you launch your way-hot bod around the campfire, and—"

"Okay, okay—" he laughed "—you went a little overboard at the end, but…" Max's voice trailed off.

Again, she seemed more interested in lusty pursuits than self-preservation, but he ignored that part. He was getting good at ignoring the things about her that drove him batty. Hell, it had to be love.

But her suggestion was way better than she knew. Because Max did happen to know about a Gypsy camp. He should have thought of it before. If only to call his good friend Gregori and ask if he knew any stories about Rajko's box.

Smiling, Max pulled the car to the shoulder of the road.

"You know what, Tink. You might just be better at treasure hunting than I gave you credit for." Then he leaned over and kissed her socks off before he turned the car around and headed northwest.

10

CASSIE LOOKED OUT THE WINDOW of their camper—the view was of another camper located about a foot away. "I pictured a band of Gypsies living differently." Max and Cassie were in a caravan park, or rather a trailer park as places like this were called in the good ol' U. S. of A.

"Sorry, shortstuff. They ditched the whole painted-wagon-in-the-woods thing with the new millennium."

She chuckled. "Shut up. You're being a pain again."

Part of Cassie didn't care where she and Max parked their tired carcasses. She was just glad to be out of the car. Russia was a wa-a-ay big place and they'd been driving forever. They'd even slept inside the cramped vehicle when they'd pulled over at a gas station along the route.

By midmorning it had been all she could do not to start whining *Are we there, yet? Are we there yet?* But now that they'd finally arrived, she had mixed feelings. While she was glad they were safe and no longer in the car, she didn't want the lover's box near anyone with woo-woo abilities. She didn't want some Gypsy psychic to pick up on its racy powers, or her usage of said racy powers.

Besides, she'd only been kidding when she'd mouthed off to Max. Truthfully, in this day and age, she'd assumed that if members of the Romani race still shared proximity it was probably because they enjoyed living near people of the same culture rather than a tribe or relations thing. Like Chinatown or Little Italy.

Well, thanks to her and her big mouth, here they were…. Since there was nothing she could do about it, however, she might as well make the best of the situation. And hopefully her concerns were nothing more than silly paranoia.

Grinning at Max, she let the gauzy curtain flutter back into place. The little neighborhood was clean, the homes well lived in, but tidy. And while these trailers might be on wheels, she doubted very seriously they'd ever been moved from their lots. So it was a good thing she hadn't expected a merry troupe of Romani wandering from village to village.

"Great." She faked a forlorn sigh. "Next you're gonna tell me that there's no Gypsy king running around here, and I won't get to have my own hot-and-heavy affair with a stud muffin like Rajko, huh?" she teased him.

Max was checking the cupboards in the kitchen, scrounging for food, and he smacked her on the fanny as she walked past. "No. You'll just have to stick with me, my tight black pants and my blousy shirt as I do the bump around the campfire. But I don't think they have those anymore, either, unless it's to roast weenies and drink beer."

"Fine. Ruin all my illusions," she said, pretending to

be disappointed. "So how did you know to come here, and how do you know Gregori?"

Gregori, a Romani gentleman who was probably in his late fifties, had welcomed Max into the fold with booming hellos and open arms when they'd arrived unannounced. His wife had been at the market, but he knew she'd be ecstatic when she heard that Max was here for a visit. What woman wouldn't be?

After settling them into his nephew's trailer—the nephew conveniently out of town—Gregori had told Max to come and go as he liked and that dinner was still at sundown.

"I came through here years ago," Max answered. "Gregori let me bunk with him and his wife while I was in the area chasing down a small amber statue for this private buyer in Germany. I already knew Gregori from when we'd both worked on a dig site over in Turkey a few years before that."

Cassie had absolutely no idea what he was talking about, but she nodded and hummed. Max definitely got around.

He shot her a grin. "But don't get too discouraged about the campfire thing. Since it's summer, our friends here cook outside a lot. There'll be wine and guitar music. And you can get your palm read when we talk to the clan *norayv*," he said.

"The clan *norayv*, huh. Who's that, the neighborhood fortune-teller? The go-to person if I need someone zapped with the evil eye? Excellent. Could come in quite handy if you turn into an obnoxious roomie."

Laughing, he shook his head. "Then I better make sure I get to her first. The *norayv* is also the clan story keeper and wise woman. All the Gypsies claim psychic powers, but the most gifted female in the tribe is chosen to be the *norayv*."

Wonderful. If there were any Gypsy stereotypes with an ounce of authenticity, why did it have to be that one? Cassie found her earlier apprehension ratcheting back up to red alert. The absolute last thing she needed was some lusty, well-preserved Esmeralda look-alike who'd blab to Max about Rajko's deluxe sex charm. Or if she wasn't already aware of the legend, be somehow able to sense the box's mucho-mojo with her psychic powers.

Well, hopefully, this *norayv,* wise woman, keeper of the legends, was really crappy at her job. And she resembled a wizened, toothless crone.

Ack! Sooner or later Max was bound to show this *norayv* the lover's box, and Cassie suddenly remembered that her flipping diary was locked inside said box. She'd been taking it in and out of the thing since they'd landed in Russia, and she needed to get it out of there pronto.

First Max would mention that he should probably study the lover's box and Cassie would scurry like a mouse, come up with some excuse to drag her backpack into the bathroom, then whip out her diary. Then Max would stare at the stupid thing like it was a Rubik's Cube, looking for secret compartments or hidden panels. Then Cassie would get nervous, fearing her voodoo hold on Max was seconds away from going kaput. Then Max would acknowledge that it was just a plain box with no hidden clues and Cassie would sneak off the second she could think of a reason and lock her diary back inside.

It was a hassle, but she had no other choice. Screw her new tough-girl skills. She'd absolutely *die* if Max ever found out that she was using the lover's box to get jiggy with him. And death by extreme humiliation was not the way she wanted to meet her final end. At the moment, however, he showed no signs of heading to the shower, taking a nap or engaging in any other activity that would allow her some alone time with the box. *Boogers*.

A brief knock sounded at the trailer's door. Before she or Max could move to open it, though, an Amazon with a bright blond cap of curls framing her face walked in. Okay, not an Amazon. She was probably only five feet nine inches, give or take, but tall enough, and slim, too—evil bitch. A real cutie-patooty, and Cassie wanted to growl like a dog defending her territory.

The giant female looked about nineteen years old, tops. She spotted Max and squealed, then said in a sexy Russian accent, "Max, you're back!" and launched herself into the gorgeous pig's arms.

Reflexes honed, no doubt, by being on the receiving end of a million such launches, he caught the long-stemmed hussy.

"Natalia? My gosh, you're all grown up. I can't believe it. You still wore braids the last time I was here." He smiled down at her, and even when the killer grin wasn't directed at her, Cassie felt its effect.

His grin was equivalent to a good thirty minutes of foreplay for other guys, the sexy jerk. Evil Natalia looked about ready to orgasm.

"Gregori told me that you were here," she gushed. "He said that you needed to talk to the *norayv,* so I trotted right over and here I am."

Wait a second! *Norayv?* The young cutie who looked like a coed was the clan's wise woman? So much for a wrinkled crone with shiny gums. *Oh, the cruel injustices of life!*

Well, blondie could trot right back to her crystal ball and shove it up her…er…where the sun don't shine when she got there. Max was Cassie's and she'd snatch every silky curlicue from the grabby gal's head if she didn't remove the hands. From Max. Now.

Besides, Cassie didn't want to perpetuate stereotypes or anything, but the blond, blue-eyed tootsie squealing and groping Max did not look like she had a drop of Romani blood. More like pints and pints of Swedish swimsuit model.

Only the tall infant's accessories resembled a Gypsy fortune-teller's: bright red silk scarf tied around the top half of her perky mop—probably covering her roots—the scarf ends dangling rakishly to one side, pirate-style. About two inches of shiny curls bounced from beneath, like a playful hair fringe. Gold hoop earrings and a bunch of jingly bracelets finished the look. The rest was vintage teenybopper: tight, low hipster jeans and a tiny crop top.

And was her flawless skin actually tan?

"You don't have to tell me a thing. I know why

you're here. I saw it in the cards," the girl said breathily to Max.

Oh, brother.

"There is danger coming for you."

Ooh, what a display of psychic powers. Like Max would be lying low in the Russian countryside because something safe was coming for him. Did people pay this child for predictions like that?

Lucky for Max he broke the vivacious leech's suction from his torso, and set her down. "Cassie, this is Natalia." Max slipped his arm around Cassie's shoulder and pulled her into his side. "Natalia's mom was the *norayv* when I was here before. But now that Natalia's reached maturity—"

Boy, had she ever…gag.

"—the clan must have voted her in," he finished. Natalia nodded, huge white teeth flashing as she smiled.

"A pleasure to meet you." Natalia held out her hand. Great. She was nice. *Ugh.*

"How do you do?" Cassie plastered a smile on her face and shook Natalia's hand. "Great scarf. Very authentic," she said, unable to help herself.

Natalia grinned sheepishly, batting at one end of the red silk. "Customers like it when they come for a reading."

"Hey, you gotta give the people their money's worth. Customer satisfaction can be a real bitch."

Max coughed, then steered Cassie toward the couch. "Have a seat," he said to Natalia. "I think I saw a jug of wine in the kitchen. I don't think Gregori's nephew will mind if we help ourselves."

Oh, fabulous idea. Get the adolescent drunk, then she'll really be crawling all over you. But Cassie kept her stupid smile frozen in place and said thanks when Max asked if she'd like a glass of vino. Sure. Bring on the liquor. Wasted was about the only way she'd get through this visit.

The camper wasn't all that big, but Max did have to go a few feet away to get to the kitchen. Cassie watched him leave. When she turned back to Natalia, the other woman was staring at her like she was looking at a bug under a microscope.

Immediately, as if there wasn't a single second to waste, Natalia leaned forward and said in a dramatic, hushed voice, "You already have what you are searching for. It has been in your possession all along."

Cassie blinked. "Wow. Just like Dorothy in *The Wizard of Oz,* eh?" Well, the girl might be easy on the eyes, but she was clearly cracked. Cassie glanced down at her sneakers. "So, I just click three times, and the treasure will drop out of my shoes?"

"You have what you are looking for. Your hunt is at an end."

"Ooh-ka-ay. I wonder what's taking Max so long? I'm gonna check and see if the big lug needs—"

"But time is running out. If you do not use your gift soon to ask for that which you truly desire—the real fantasy of your heart—then it will be too late…."

"—some help, and—hey, wait a minute. What did you just say?"

"Here you go." Max was carrying their glasses. He

was also insanely sexy. Ever the gentleman, he kept the pecking order clear—hopefully going by sexual preference, not age—and handed Cassie hers first.

Cassie lifted her wine to her mouth and took a healthy gulp. What the hell had just happened? Had blondie just told her to ask for the true *fantasy* of her heart or was Cassie losing it? Cripes. Maybe the bimbette really was psychic.

One word to Max about Cassie using the lover's box, however, and she would rip out one of Natalia's gold hoops and shove it up the Gypsy chick's nose. Cassie's hand shook as she tipped back her glass. Max gave her a funny look that said, *When the heck did you turn into a lush?*

Cassie ignored him. The little hairs at the back of her neck were tingling. Something very weird had just happened with Natalia.

Max lowered himself onto the couch, sitting next to Cassie, their thighs touching, but she was too freaked out to enjoy the buzz. Instead, she barely spared him a glance and went straight back to worrying. Of course, Natalia had kept with the typical cryptic-fortune-telling MO and could have been talking about one of a dozen different possibilities. Not that Cassie could think of any, besides the obvious, but still it warranted mentioning, right?

Meanwhile, Max and Natalia were yakking it up. "Listen, while you're here, I want you to look at something." Max stood and went into the camper's bedroom, and Cassie almost swallowed her tongue.

Holy moly, Max was already trying to show Natalia the box and the jig was about to go belly-up right here and now. The tall, evil cutie's predictions were coming true right before Cassie's eyes. Or at least the part of her spiel about it *soon* being *too late* for Cassie to ask for the *real fantasy of her heart.*

Rats. Well…it had certainly been *soon,* all right. She'd been given the equivalent of a psychic thirty-second warning. Natalia might speak to the spirit world but she wasn't very helpful.

Before Cassie could jump off the couch, blow this Popsicle stand and hoof it to Siberia, Max was back and handing Stasi's diary, not the lover's box, to the tall and perky *norayv.*

Cassie almost passed out with relief, and Max was looking at her funny again.

"You okay, Tink?"

Cassie narrowed her eyes, her anxiety—then massive relief—momentarily swamped by annoyance. Must he make short jokes in front of the Amazon?

Max grinned as if he could read her thoughts, and she sniffed and said, "Just peachy, thanks."

Natalia gasped when her hands touched the diary. "This book is the source of your danger. Or half of the whole."

Cassie had already finished her own glass of wine and she reached for Max's and polished his off, too. "Yeah, yeah, we got that without a call to the Psychic Hotline. Now how about some info we can use."

Max made a choking noise, then scowled ferociously at Cassie.

Natalia lifted her chin. "I can only tell what I receive."

Again, whatever the hell *that* meant. It was like chitchatting with Yoda. *Danger there is much of. Come for you the dark side will. Blah, blah, blah...* With Natalia's track record, she'd probably announce that Cassie and Max were going to die, but not tell them when.

Natalia blinked her huge baby blues. "Other than great, great pleasure the past is not what I hear from this book but rather the future. Powerful men." She frowned, her voice sounding as if she were going into a trance. "They do not want her identity known. The woman who penned this was supposed to have died. They do not want proof of her escape to surface. They want to cover the truth, but their success is...unclear...."

Then with the drama of someone far beyond her years, she stood and swayed, her fingers rubbing her temples. "I must rest. You have another piece of the puzzle. Bring it to me after the moon has risen full and sits in the center of the sky. No sooner." Then she gave a quick wave, and said, "See you guys at dinner."

Wow, Broadway was missing a star with Natalia stuck out here in the boondocks. And Max hadn't even gotten a chance for a Q & A about Rajko and Stasi before the big, blond Gypsy had bopped out of here. Not that Cassie particularly gave a rip.

Max ran his fingers through his hair, light shining off the golden streaks. "Damn. That was not what I was hoping to hear." He plopped back down beside her on the dinky sofa, his legs sprawling in a *V.* Staring into the distance—well, into the pressboard paneling—he absently stroked his hand up and down her leg from groin to knee, and her heart went pitter-patter.

"You mean the o' wise Natalia's prediction, or her blatant attempt to hook up with you when the moon reaches its zenith in the night sky?" she mimicked.

His lips twitched. "Feisty, bloodthirsty and jealous. Quit giving me grief, peanut. When you're in the room, there's no other gal for me." His fingers squeezed, then went back to their meandering path. She briefly wondered if opening her thighs so he had more room to maneuver would come across as slutty.

"Huh. Interesting word choice you picked there. 'When I'm in the room,'" she repeated, although she was unable to work up any real venom. Like an alligator getting its belly rubbed, Cassie was calmed by his touch.

"You're always in the room. You haven't left my side for three days." Which technically wasn't true, but pretty close.

"Okay," he muttered, working the problem out loud. "Obviously Natalia's dangerous men are the FSS. And Ivan's not going to give up. Which sucks." He closed his eyes, his head dropping to the back of the couch. "It's the *cover the truth* shit that has me ready to pack up the diary and the box and special-deliver them both off to Victor's house. If I can find some proof of what I think Natalia's saying, then we're done, peanut. Over and out. I'm not messing around this time."

"Oh, you're not going to let her gloom-and-doom act get in our way, are you? I thought you were only talking to her because you wanted to know if she had any clan stories. Besides, you're not the kind of guy to believe in Gypsy hocus-pocus. I want to keep the box, it's—"

He rolled his head; their gazes locked when he lifted his lids. "I don't disbelieve. Especially, when the message comes from a Gypsy. But I don't need Natalia to tell me what I already suspected. If the FSS is trying to cover the truth, then it's dangerous. It's not worth risking your body over."

"But—"

"No. It's a very hot body." His hand slid higher until the side of his fingers pressed intimately between her legs. "I'm not done with it and I don't plan to be…for a long, long while."

Cassie gulped. Hey, no rush. He could keep her as long as he liked! But she doubted that he'd still be interested without Rajko's charm and the lover's box fueling her fantasies. She couldn't afford the risk, and she was back to her kung fu–grip plan.

"Uh…um…what about the, uh…treasure?" she finally managed. He was doing something very tricky with just his pinky. The man was gifted. There was no denying it.

He'd sidled closer, never looking away. Their eyelashes were practically butterfly kissing and his arm was heavy and warm…and busy….

"At dinner I'll find out if Natalia knows any legends I haven't heard before." His mouth had neared until his lips moved against hers when he spoke. Her every breath came straight from his mouth, warm and intoxicating, as if she needed him in order to live.

"I'll show her the box tonight, see if she gets another psychic reading. But if it's bad news, and Ivan Petrutrio is involved, the treasure is a nonissue. We don't need it. Not at that price."

Speak for yourself, she wanted to rail in frustration. She definitely needed the lover's box. For the rest of her life. She didn't want to lose Max Stone. Not yet. "But—"

He shushed her, his mouth sliding over hers. His kiss was different this time. Like the one he'd given her outside Victor's house right before he'd gone to get Stasi's diary. Her heart skipped a beat, then started thumping out of control. He was telling her things with this kiss and she was scared to believe the message.

She'd gotten this so wrong before, with Ron, and he'd been nothing compared to Max. What if she believed, trusted, and she ended up alone again? The pain would be too great this time… She wouldn't be able to recover.

He melted into her, breaking the kiss but curling her closer and sliding her around in his arms. He'd moved them down until they were lying sideways, her back to his front. She was spooned in the cradle of his chest and legs. She felt protected and sheltered yet bound to him in ways that terrified her.

"I don't want to argue. I just want to hold you," he rasped against the shell of her ear, trying to soothe her. "Maybe I'm wrong and Ivan was at Victor's for some other reason." But as she relaxed into his hold, she knew he didn't believe that.

Yet if Cassie wanted to stay in control of her future, she needed to keep the box. She couldn't lose it. Then the annoying Gypsy's words came back to her... *"Time is running out."* If she didn't use her gift soon and ask for the real fantasy of her heart, it would be too late....

While Cassie chewed on her lip and plotted, she eventually noticed that Max's breathing had changed. He'd fallen asleep. Well, he had to be exhausted. They'd done nothing but run from bad guys and boink. Tentatively, she slipped from his arms. He grumbled, but was out for the count. She stared down at him for a second and her eyes began to sting, her vision blurring with moisture.

Just looking at him hurt. He was everything she'd ever dreamed of, exactly what she'd asked for when she'd written out her first fantasy...but the reality of him was so much more. More than a stunning face and fabulous bedroom skills.

Max was brave and smart. He laughed when she mouthed off and thought she was funny. He listened to her and appeared to be fascinated with everything she did and said. He seemed to genuinely like her and didn't pick her apart but, rather, built her up. And he was a total warrior, willing to do anything to keep her safe...even give up the treasure.

Smiling sadly, she turned away and walked into the bedroom. She knelt by her backpack. In the past few days, Cassie had learned to accept the unbelievable. So it was silly to admit that the sex charm really worked, yet brush off Natalia's powers as bogus and ignore her warnings.

She took out the lover's box and traced the gaudy swirls of paint. Maybe the vulgar colors were a reminder of the jewels Stasi had stolen and brought with her when she'd run off with her Gypsy king. A constant reminder that no treasure was worth more than what Rajko's charm could give her when she'd written out her fantasies and locked them inside…or worth more than the love they'd found in each other's arms….

And that's what Cassie truly desired. Not wild porn-movie reenactments, or S and M role-playing. She wanted to make *love* with Max. Before it was too late.

Cassie found a pen, then removed her diary and wrote out one last fantasy. The one of her heart….

11

WELL, THE GODDESS had gotten her campfire and Max had even danced. He'd had to with the way the young bucks living in the caravan park had shown off for her, pulling out all the stops. One in particular had seemed intent on impressing Cassie. When she'd commented to Natalia that the idiot resembled a young Johnny Depp, he'd had enough. At least Max hadn't been rigged up in tight black pants and a blousy shirt. Though he did know some of the traditional steps and was good at them. They were sort of like martial arts but rowdier.

Of course, Johnny Depp junior had been wearing black jeans and some billowy red thing and Cassie had nearly swooned her approval. But Max didn't want to think about that. If he didn't suspect that she was mostly trying to pay him back over the way Natalia kept cornering him to talk about Rajko, Max would've strangled her by now. He hadn't kept her alive and out of trouble on two continents only to watch her drool over some young Gypsy stud.

Well, the Gypsy lothario could go find his own goddess to drive him nuts. The pixie brat was Max's, and from now on all drooling would be reserved for him.

Scowling, Max unlaced his boots and kicked them off. They were back in the camper and he wanted nothing more than to take the goddess to bed until, as Cassie had earlier mocked, the moon was at its zenith in the sky.

"Don't you think Natalia's reaction was a little over the top when I mentioned that Stasi sometimes signed the diary as Krasili?"

"Well, Natalia has a bit of a flair that way. And, according to her, Stasi was never called Krasili in any of their tales. Apparently, it means 'queen' or 'princess.' Since Stasi was *gadje,* not Gypsy, she couldn't be the Krasili." He shrugged. "Something like that, anyway."

Cassie huffed. "Rajko was their king. So what's the big whoop that Stasi occasionally penned off as the queen? Natalia is a dingbat, I tell you. I don't think you should trust her. Maybe you should only deal with her mom from now on."

Nope, Natalia was not Cassie's favorite person, and Max stomped down hard on the laugh working its way up. "Aw, Natalia's not so bad." Then just to really rile her up, he said, "She sure has grown up to be a real looker, though."

"Hmm…" Cassie pretended to study her fingernails, the first time in three days he'd ever seen her give them notice. "I guess if you want to be loomed over. Those high heels of hers were totally inappropriate for outdoor dining. I felt like I was standing next to a tree. But I suppose if you go for that type, she's okay." The goddess shrugged, then added, "Now if you want to talk about a looker, how about that guy in the red shirt tonight." Her voice became dreamy. "He's my idea of—"

"I don't remember," Max interrupted, cutting her off. "But the Krasili thing raises an interesting point," he hurried on. "Maybe Stasi really was an aristocrat before the revolution. That would mean that one of my father's theories was right."

Cassie fell back on the bed laughing at his abrupt, not-so-subtle change of topic. He ignored this and took off his shirt, then rolled toward her. They were alone. In a bed. Safe for now. Good Lord, he was going to devour her….

She smiled up at him, her eyes sparkling. "I've got an even better theory. Listen, she signed her name Krasili for at least the last half of the diary but somehow the nickname never makes it into Gypsy history. What if that's because she was more than just an ordinary aristocrat? What if she was royalty?"

Max barely registered her words. She looked so beautiful and happy. He wanted to keep her that way. He wanted… *He wanted to keep her*… The realization hit him like a fist slammed into his gut.

The back of his eyes felt hot as he stared into her face. It was hard to breathe; bands of tension were squeezing beneath his ribs. Things were misfiring in his brain, circuits blowing. At once the room seemed too bright and he watched her through a blur of emotion.

She asked him another question and he shook his head, dazed. He couldn't talk. Things he'd never allowed himself to feel were rushing on too strong. It was as if, after a lifetime of being alone and *not* caring, he intensely cared for, and about, every facet of this wonderful woman.

And then her expression changed and she gave him that soft smile of hers and he thought, *This is it. She's the one. I cannot lose her. Lose this feeling.* He didn't ever want to be alone, or be without her. The past didn't matter. He could trust in her, trust in them, together.

Pain he hadn't even been aware of at his father's betrayal washed free. He had to blink fast, afraid he was going to cry. But even if he did, he felt safe with Cassie. Somehow she knew him, really knew him at a core level. She'd always believe in him. And with her, nothing could ever hurt him again.

His hand trembled as he brushed back her hair, then he did something he'd never done before.

He made love to a woman—because he'd fallen ass over heels in love with Cassie Parker....

"I DON'T SEE WHY NATALIA can't just look at the diary in the daytime like a normal person."

Max jumped down the camper's three metal steps. He walked over to Cassie and took her hand. He couldn't stop touching her now that he'd admitted to himself that he loved her. Though he hadn't told her yet.

Every time he tried to say the words they got stuck in his throat. Not because he didn't mean them, but because he meant them too much. It was too new. Too raw. But there was plenty of time. He had the rest of his life to tell her. Every day if he wanted, which he did. Just not yet…

And while she hadn't said the words to him, either, he knew she loved him back. She'd cried at the end there and he understood why. Her climax had been a culmination of more than just the physical. It had been the most stunning moment of his life…intoxicating, addicting, and he wanted to keep feeling the high again and again. No relic, no hunt, nothing, had ever given him a rush like making love to the goddess. And from now on he planned to live for a whole different kind of adrenaline hit.

But all he said was, "You could have stayed in bed if you wanted. I don't mind." He kissed the back of her hand, then gave it a quick squeeze.

Cassie snorted. "Your girlfriend would have liked that a little too much."

Max laughed and bumped her hip with his as they walked away from the trailer. Natalia had said to meet at the wooden tables where they'd had dinner—basically a picnic area and a fire pit out in the woods. Apparently, the location suited her melodramatic leanings.

Cassie was still grumbling about something, her backpack slung over one shoulder and her hair adorably disheveled, as if she'd just crawled out of bed—which she had. There had been no way in hell his jealous little goddess was going to let him talk with Natalia alone. This was fine with him since he never wanted to be alone with anyone but Cassie.

He'd also let her carry the lover's box inside her stupid pack. For some reason it riled her up when she wasn't the one lugging it around and it hadn't mattered to him one way or another. No one would track them down out here.

"Hey, about the Krasili thing. You distracted me when I mentioned it earlier," she said, and the muscles in his stomach jerked at the memory of how they'd both been *distracted*. "But I was thinking about your dad's theory, and this high-up FSS guy."

"Uh-huh." Max was barely listening. She was so damn adorable, it hurt to watch her. His heart squeezed. She dazzled him. Took his breath away.

"Well, the FSS is sort of like the CIA, right?"

He grinned. "Your grasp of international affairs is inspiring."

"Shut up." She stuck her sexy, pink tongue out at him and he cracked up. "Anyhow, so the FSS acts for the Russian government, correct? I mean, like, with this whole cover-up, conspiracy theory, or whatever you wanna call it, that nutty Natalia alluded to in typical cryptic o'-great-psychic-babble MO—"

"What?" He really didn't care, but she was cute when she was on a rant so he egged her on.

"Modus operandi."

He forced himself not to crack a smile. "I knew that part. It was at the 'cryptic psychic babble' part that you lost me."

"Oh." She waved her free hand around in a flap of annoyance. "The whole, you-are-safe-but-there-is-danger thing. Bad men are coming, but their success is unclear. Yeesh."

"Natalia had a couple of helpful tips. She's got a gift. I think she's very talented." He kept pressing Cassie's buttons just for the hell of it.

"Two. She said two things that were helpful. I was addressing them, but you interrupted. Quit trying to wind me up." Laughing, Max ducked her slap to his shoulder.

Lord, he was having fun. He'd never done this. Walked in the dark, swinging hands like a kid with the woman he loved. Hell, he was turning into a Hallmark card. And he didn't care.

"Okay," she said. "If the Kremlin wanted something kept secret, then it would be the FSS who'd take care of it, right?"

"Yep."

"So, with your father's theory that Stasi was an aristocrat on the run, and Natalia's government cover-up comment, I was thinking—"

"Uh… Oh… It's always hard when you first start, but with practice this thinking stuff gets easier." Max dodged another slap.

"Who would the government still care about after all this time? What if Stasi wasn't merely an aristocrat but royalty? What woman of royal birth, who was alive around the time of the Russian Revolution, would be so important that anyone would give a rip anymore? What woman has so fascinated the public at large with the rumor that she didn't really die. That she escaped her execution because she had a fortune of jewels sewn into the lining of her dress, and—"

"Who also had a half-dozen movies made about her shocking reappearance, including a cartoon with a funny-looking bat for a sidekick? I know where you're going with this. If you say Anastasia, I'll…well…I don't know what I'll do. But I'll be really annoyed because you'll get all excited and it'll take me forever to talk you down. It's a waste of time, Tink. Where would Anastasia meet a Gypsy king?"

"The bat was Rasputin's sidekick. And how the heck should I know where they met? Maybe Rajko worked in the palace stables. Where would any woman with a title meet a Gypsy king? But it doesn't matter, since they did meet and lived happily ever after."

"Lucky them," he muttered. "No matter who Stasi was, I bet Rajko didn't have to put up with the kind of crap that I do."

"Quit your whining. It's the perfect explanation for how Rajko ended up with a bunch of jewels. I can prove I'm right. I think." Cassie freed her hand and Max sighed. She swung her backpack around to her front and started rummaging around inside. "I noticed something before when I was looking at the lover's box. The paint on the box isn't just a random pattern. There's an emblem and when you see it I expect groveling. Lots of groveling," she said.

"Hey, Tink, be careful. Wait till we get there before you start flapping the box around. After everything I've been through because of that tacky-looking antique, I'll kill you if you break it before I figure out what the hell it all means."

He cupped her palm back against his and started yanking her toward the picnic tables that he could finally see up ahead. He wanted to be sitting down when he heard the rest of her asinine theories. "You've been reading too many romance novels," he said. "The whole idea is stupid. The Czar of Russia's teenage daughter, which would have made her a grand duchess, by the way, did not run off with Rajko and live out the rest of her life with the Gypsies. Talk about slumming it."

"First, a girl can never read too many romance novels. And second, says you."

"Yes. That's exactly what I say. I say, wait—huh?" How come he always lost the thread of their convoluted conversations, but she was ready with the volleys like a legal defense team?

"Listen, it makes sense. Stasi is obviously a diminutive of Anastasia."

"Pure coincidence. And how about I start calling you *Ass?* It's a *diminutive* of Cassie." They were almost at the edge of the camp now, but he didn't see Natalia waiting for them as he'd expected.

"No. But you can kiss mine," she shot back, then said as if he hadn't spoken, "It also explains why nobody called her Krasili. She'd be too nervous that someone might make the connection."

"Oh, brother. That has got to be your weakest point yet. Listen. I get that you think it would be cool for Anastasia to have made it out alive and spent the rest of her years making whoopee with Rajko. But it's too much. The Bolsheviks would never have let her live. Hell, they slaughtered her whole family. Archeologists found the grave site more than a decade ago and the government had DNA testing done on the bones. Then they reburied them in a big funeral."

"Two of the children were missing. The boy Alexi and a girl, either Mari or Anastasia. So there."

"Okay, so we watched the same documentary. It's still a stupid idea and only conspiracy-theory freaks think that any of the Romanovs made it out of Ipatiev House alive."

"What about conspiracy freaks with the FSS on their tail? What do they think?"

"They think you're getting as sensational as Natalia."

"I don't believe it. A disparaging word about the giant Gypsy girl."

Jealous *and* sarcastic. At least the goddess was consistent. Max narrowed his eyes and scanned the tree line. Where the heck was Natalia? He didn't mean to be a jerk, but usually when a woman planned a rendezvous with him, she showed up. Early. And while it was her own stupid flair for dramatics that had made her choose to meet him at the edge of the woods in the middle of the night, Natalia was barely out of her teens. She was young and alone.

Not liking his sudden uneasiness, he started dragging Cassie along faster. She kept yapping, clutching her backpack in one arm, the lover's box shining eerily in the moonlight through the still-open flap.

"And who the heck would think to look for Anastasia with a band of Gypsies? No one, I tell you, that's who. She found the perfect hiding place and—"

A loud, ominous click broke the night's silence. Well, the silence other than Cassie's jabbering. Max's feet came to a dead stop, almost wrenching Cassie's arm from the socket when she kept walking.

"Hey—" Her voice cut off in a squeak when a man stepped from the shadows, gripping Natalia's arm, a gun pointed at the young Gypsy's head.

"You shouldn't argue with your new lover, Max. She's actually right."

"I am? I mean, yeah, I am," Cassie said, subtly trying to shift herself between Max and the ass-wipe with the gun. She was an idiot. A sweet one, but still an idiot and Max jerked her back toward him.

"Hey, Vic. How's it hangin'?" The ass-wipe, of course, was Victor Hofford. He couldn't believe that one of Vic's men had tailed them here. Lord, Max was really going to have to do something about Vic.

"The box and the diary. Now. Or the girl dies." Victor pressed the muzzle of the gun against Natalia's temple. The other man was short and Natalia was a long drink of water, so it was a slight reach.

"You should've worn your lifts for this gig," Max said while his brain scrambled for a plan. How the hell had Victor tracked them to Gregori's camp? "And when did you turn into a killer? You've always been a putz but you've never stooped to outright murder."

Max scored a direct hit with the height crack.

Victor's nostrils flared, the whites of his eyes a quick flash in the moonlight. However, the murder taunt was like water off a duck's back.

Max would've handed over the lover's box in a heartbeat. His desire to beat Victor to the treasure wasn't worth Natalia's life or Cassie's. But he suspected that the goddess was going to be a major snag. The girl just plain wasn't reasonable when it came to parting with the lover's box.

Victor solved the puzzle of why he was suddenly stooping to outright acts of violence. And it was a lulu. "I'd kill quite a few people when the rewards are this great."

Max assumed Vic was referring to the treasure. "Feeling the recession, huh? Hey, man, times are tough. Why don't you cut back on your guards? That should free up some money. They're not very good, anyway. I waltzed in, right under their noses, and got the diary without a single snag."

While Victor answered—Max was surprised his keep-the-villain-talking scheme was actually working—Max slowly stepped in front of Cassie. Or he tried to, anyway. She kept shifting forward and if she didn't cut it out, she'd scooch them right up into Victor's grill.

"The world will finally give me the recognition I deserve when I prove that Anastasia escaped the bloodbath and lived out the rest of her existence as the Gypsy king's lover," Victor said, with a grim smile. "The fallout will be enormous for the Russians, of course, since they insist the whole family is dead. But I will be famous."

Great. Max was surrounded by kooks. The only

thing left was for Victor to break out in a maniacal laugh. "So, did some Internet site tip you off?"

"No. Not the Internet. It was your father who discovered the truth. He always believed that Rajko's woman was the grand duchess. Didn't he tell you?"

His father had obviously left out that part. But, finally, with Cassie in his life, Max no longer cared about his crummy past with his dead father. He laughed and said, "He knew better. I'd have laughed in his face. But I have to question the source. My father never had an original idea."

He glanced at Natalia. She stood as still as a statue, her huge eyes fixed on Max. She was being enormously brave, the fact that she towered over her assailant possibly a small comfort in spite of the gun.

Victor smiled slowly and Max had a moment's unease. "Remember when you accused me of selling stolen relics, then took off in a blaze of wrath?" No. Max didn't remember the blaze of wrath part but whatever. Victor said, "Your father eventually put two and two together."

Max cocked his head. "You mean he knew you were guilty?" He should be feeling vindicated but, again, he no longer cared. And not in a cocky, defensive way. He was just plain indifferent. Besides, his mind was too busy racing over possible ways to get Cassie and Natalia out of there safely. If Victor was expecting him to freak out, he was bound to be disappointed.

"Yes, he knew. And didn't care. He eventually began a few small ventures into the market himself." Victor paused, waiting. "What, no insults? Where's your laughter now, Max?"

Max just sighed. He'd moved on and no longer needed validation from his dead father. He'd have shared the good news with Vic, but that would've really thrown a wrench in the little guy's plans.

Victor scowled. "Fine. Believe me or don't, it doesn't matter. Your father always needed money. You know more than anyone how he was. He justified his actions by claiming he was selling off lesser artifacts to fund more excavations."

There was a ring of truth to Vic's words, but even this didn't anger Max as he might have expected. But shock the "fugg" out of him? Yes.

"It was one of his contacts here in Russia, a man inside the old government's regime, who told your father what really happened to the royal family that night," Victor explained.

"Your father rightly suspected that, if the box was ever found, the Russian government would be willing to pay an exorbitant fee to keep the secret. It was an excellent idea and I've already suggested it to Ivan Petrutrio. If he meets my demands, Anastasia's secret will stay just that. And the present parties in power will be safe from any pesky royalists trying to bring back the old regime."

Max cracked up despite the danger of the situation. "It'll never happen. And you're an even bigger idiot than I thought if you're trying to blackmail Petrutrio."

"I agree," another voice spoke out, and Ivan Petrutrio stepped from the shadows, his gun drawn. "By the way," Ivan rumbled in his thick accent, "there's no old regime. It's the same, only better. And far, far more efficient in dealing with those who threaten the country's safety."

Max whipped his head around and, almost simulta-neously, Cassie tried to jump in front of him. Ivan's arm and the aim of his gun swung to her and Max stopped thinking like a normal human being. He stepped in, turning his body toward hers and swept her leg out.

As they started falling, he saw that Natalia had used the diversion to haul off and wallop Victor a good one. She was a big girl and Victor had been staring at Ivan when her blow struck his face.

Meanwhile, Max landed on top of Cassie, covering as much of her as possible and praying he'd stop any bullet from reaching her. But instead of the crack of gunfire, he heard an ominous crunch of wood. Pulling up enough to look into her eyes, he met her astonished gaze. *Hell.* If he wasn't mistaken, the goddess had just managed to land on her backpack and crush the box underneath her.

He quickly looked toward Ivan, the biggest threat present. Ivan had knocked Victor's gun aside. Victor was frozen, hands in the air as if he was afraid to breathe the wrong way. *Good.* Also, Natalia was inching away and Ivan was letting her.

Ivan started talking to Victor, his voice low and ugly. While the pair was occupied, Max used the opportunity to roll to Cassie's side, keeping himself between her and Ivan. Cassie's expression was horrified rather than scared, and she quickly shrugged off her backpack and scrambled upright.

Pieces of wood were spilling out the top of the pack. But that's not what made Max's spine almost snap because he straightened so fast. A half-dozen stones glittered in the meager light from where they'd spilled onto the dirt. Max gaped. So did Cassie.

Holy shit. The goddess had found the treasure. When she'd smashed the box beneath, her...er...backside, she'd set the jewels somehow hidden inside free. No secret compartment here, though. Apparently the only way to find the treasure was to destroy the box.

Time seemed to stand still. Max stared down at the ground, then shook his head and it was like being released from a trance.

Cassie dropped to her knees over the carnage, muttering a list of vile curses and frantically trying to scoop everything into her pack. Insanely she seemed just as concerned about retrieving the splinters of wood as the shiny objects sprinkled around their feet. *What the hell?*

But Max's priorities were now crystal clear in his mind, as if he'd suddenly woken from a dream. Cassie wasn't running the show anymore and he was finally putting his foot down. Literally. Max stepped onto her backpack, the fabric under the sole of his boot. He didn't want her grabbing her pack and he didn't want Ivan turning his attention their way. "Are you insane?" He darted a telling glance toward Ivan and Victor. "It's too late for that now. It's over."

Cassie gasped and fell back, hitting her bottom on

the ground. "Too late?" She sounded appalled. "Wha—"

"Do you really think Ivan is going to let you take anything out of here? It's done now. Get a grip, Cassie. There's nothing in there worth dying over."

Shockingly, tears splashed down onto her cheeks, her devastation instantaneous. "But we, I mean I need—"

"Cassie, stop," he hissed. She was far more upset than he'd have expected, but he couldn't figure it out now. "You have to leave. Go. Right now. For once this isn't about what you want, it's—"

She gave a sharp cry and jerked away as if he'd struck her, and Max suddenly had a bad feeling that they were talking about two different things. But he didn't have time for this. Not only was Cassie in danger, but Natalia was, too.

Cassie was small and it was dark, so when she whirled to flee it took him a moment to track the movement. Then he spotted her; she'd veered toward Ivan and Victor as she turned to escape. *Oh, crap.*

Max started to lunge, his arms outstretched and his mouth forming around a frantic *no*. But he was already too late; her leg was swinging out and behind Victor as if she were making a quick soccer goal before she hit the road.

Her foot hit up under Vic's backside, between his legs, racking him in the balls. In one smooth motion she followed through, then broke into a run.

As Cassie disappeared into the dark, Victor howled, taken totally unaware. His body flew forward from the force of Cassie's ball-buster, automatically curling into the classic post–hit-in-the-nads pose. Ivan's gun went off, but Victor's position meant the bullet missed his head. Too bad.

This was Max's last thought before all hell broke loose. When it was finally over, he'd remember that his last glimpse of Cassie Parker had been with tears welling from her eyes like jewels spilling across the ground.

CASSIE FINISHED PACKING her last box. She'd been back in Florida for two weeks, but she was leaving again.

Watching Max wake from the spell of the lover's box as if he'd been dashed in the face with a bucket of cold water was in many ways the worst moment of her life. One second he'd been looking at her with love and then—boom—he just…wasn't. Devastation did not begin to describe the pain. She'd felt so helpless and angry. Her biggest fear had come true—she'd lost Max.

She barely remembered leaving the clearing and darting into the woods. Behind the line of trees, tears running down her cheeks, she'd watched the chaos left in the wake of her departure. Once Ivan had finally cuffed Victor, the FSS officer had holstered his gun and turned to Max. Max might have had some fast talking to do, but his life was no longer in imminent danger.

Of course, the ever-beautiful Natalia had thrown herself against Max, collapsing gently in his strong arms. The other woman's awesome bravery had conveniently disappeared once the worst was over. Afraid that Max would look over and see her crying her heart out, Cassie had turned and run to the trailer. She'd stopped only long enough to grab her passport and a few other items, then snatched her car keys and left.

She'd felt as though she'd never stop crying as she'd pictured Max shaking his head as if he was waking from a dream. Staring at her as if he were seeing her for the first time. He'd even called her Cassie. Twice… There'd been no point sticking around after that.

She'd driven numbly, physically and emotionally exhausted. Then, halfway back to St. Petersburg, images of her attack on Victor had started flashing through her mind. Her hands had gripped the wheel while she'd stilled in her seat. As if she were watching a scene in a movie, she'd been able to see herself kicking Vic's balls halfway up to his throat. Sniffing noisily, she'd sputtered out a laugh. Then, laughing even harder, Cassie had realized the truth: that she was a real live kick-ass heroine in the most literal sense of the term. *Woo-hoo!*

As she'd snickered and cried, she'd further realized something else: she might need the lover's box to get Max Stone into her bed, but she could manage the rest just fine by herself. Because the box had already been turned to toothpicks via contact with her big fat butt when she'd opened up a can of whoop on Victor. Meaning that Cassie had been acting on her own, not egged on by Gypsy mojo. She'd also been the one to find the treasure.

Not bad for the nonadventurous Parker female. At this point Cassie had started to face some home truths and she'd recognized that she was every bit as capable and daring as the other gals in her illustrious family tree. Okay, total *Wizard of Oz* moment, but, as Natalia had suggested, she'd had what she'd been looking for all along.

If only she'd been able to keep Max along with her newly acknowledged tough-girl skills…. She might not have gotten the guy, but there *had* been an interesting new development. While Cassie was gone, a buyer had contacted the store, requesting Minerva to track down a coin rumored to have been minted with the faces of Caesar and Cleopatra, a gift from Caesar to the queen he'd conquered and loved.

Legend claimed that Napoleon then discovered the coin when he'd invaded Egypt. The coin had been placed on a solid gold necklace and given to his one true love, Josephine. Legend also held that only a woman truly loved by a man could wear the coin around her neck. Frankly, Cassie had had her fill of romantic legends and mystical powers, but chasing after the coin was better than hanging around the place with only her old best friends power-napping and eating to keep her company.

She'd done this once already because of Ron. She needed a whole different kind of therapy to recover from the desolation of losing Max Stone. If she kept busy enough, then hopefully she'd stop thinking about Max. There were times when the pain nearly overwhelmed her and she could hardly bear it.

Fortunately, Minerva was unavailable, so there was no one else to take the job. The ever-crazy woman was off in South America, studying the lost civilization of the zanzawoobee, or something like that. Before Cassie had come to live here, the shop below had been open only when Minerva was in town, so her great-aunt was fine with leaving it closed until Cassie returned. Minerva hardly needed the money—the store was mostly just a place for Minerva to show off what she'd picked up in her travels.

Her great-aunt had yet to admit that she'd stolen the lover's box from Max before she sent it to Cassie. But it didn't matter anymore.

Whatever Minerva's crazy scheme, it had been worth it. Though Cassie was alone again, she felt so different than she had after her breakup with Ron. She might not ever again find the kind of love that she'd felt for Max, but she wanted to be happy. Not hide and nurse her wounds. She wanted to wake up and look forward to each day.

She was attractive and men found her sexy. Not all of them, but some of them, thank God. Ron was an ass, and she wasn't going to let him have any more impact on how she lived.

She didn't know what the future held, but it was up to her to find out. On her own, yes, but… At least with the lover's box destroyed, she'd never have to worry about someone wanting her for anything other than herself.

She looked around the room. It was quiet in the house. Empty. The teenage boy from next door was obviously one twisted kid, because he'd agreed to watch Creature until whenever Cassie returned. As if he'd heard her thoughts, the wretched feline stalked past her, reaching out a claw and making a quick slash across her ankle before he bolted. Rotten cat.

Cassie was tired. She decided to take a bath before going to bed. She had a long trip ahead of her. Tomorrow she would fly to France, then go on from there to wherever the hunt for the coin led.

Lying back in the water, she closed her eyes with a deep sigh. She hoped this wouldn't be another night when she saw the beautiful Max Stone and the lover's box in her sleep. Pushing the thoughts away, she plucked her sponge from the dish and squirted it with soap. She lazily ran it across her stomach and down her leg, pointing her toes toward the ceiling.

While she usually wasn't the queen of healthy body image, she had to admit that she was looking fine. She'd been too depressed to eat. The only good thing to come of post–traumatic Max Stone disorder was that she was back in her skinny jeans. Too bad he'd never see her in them. Well, some other lucky guy would. Eventually. Like in a year or two…when she could think of another man without feeling ill.

Who was she trying to kid? She'd be lucky to be over Max within a decade.

The clatter of breaking glass shattered her peacefully depressing moment. Her eyes flew open and she shot upright, her spine snapping to military attention.

Before she could even think to weigh the risks or

consider the dangers, she leaped from the tub, grabbed a towel and took off at a sprint. Her arms windmilling and her wet feet scrambling for purchase, she careened into the shop, trying to stop. Her hand smacked the overhead light switch. A slow tremble pervaded her limbs and she blinked rapidly, trying to adjust to the sudden light.

Then her vision came into focus and Cassie couldn't help it. She gawked just as she had the first time she'd laid eyes on Max Stone. There he was, in all his magnificent splendor, leaning back against the stuffed water buffalo. His shirt was off, just like last time, and he carried a plain wooden box—the same size as the lover's box—in his hands. It had a big red bow on top.

Her mouth worked silently then finally she found her voice. "You're here. But why?"

His definitive bad-boy grin curved wickedly across his mouth. "I salvaged your diary from the crushed remains of Rajko's box. You've got some wild fantasies going on in your head. Reading them was almost as fun as doing them."

Her hands flew up to her face, pressing against her hot cheeks as she groaned. "I forgot, I mean, I—" She broke off. Oh, jeez, she'd totally forgotten that she'd left her diary behind. Men with guns or not, she'd have run back in a flash if she'd remembered it. Anything to avoid this horrible level of embarrassment.

Oh, so what? So he'd read her fantasies. Last time she'd seen him, things had been totally whacked on the bad-guy front, and Max had been free from the Gypsy charm, and he was really here, safe and whole and alive. "But you're not mad? I thought you'd be angry because I'd used Gypsy magic to get you into bed."

Max laughed, interrupting her. "Hell, no. I'm all for it." He tapped a finger on the lid of the new lover's box, the wood gleaming brightly. No paint. "I liked the first one so much, I brought you another to replace it."

Cassie blinked. "Does it, uh…"

Max nodded, his smile growing wider. "Yep. Works just like the one Rajko made for Stasi. Your diary's waiting inside. I don't have a pen on me, but if you tell me where to find one, I'll do a fifty-yard dash."

Cassie couldn't help giggling. "But why would you do that? I mean, when it broke, you seemed so happy to be free…so relieved, but angry."

Max raised his eyebrows. "Wow. You could read all that, huh? In the dark, at gunpoint, in less than ten seconds?" He scowled. "By the way, when I told you to run, I didn't mean all the way back to Florida. You have no idea what I went through when I learned you were gone."

Cassie's forehead creased with lines and she played with the edge of her towel. She hated to relive any of the emotional pain, but she really needed to know. "But you called me Cassie—twice. The second the box broke you started using my regular name. And you told me that there was nothing in the backpack worth—"

He'd been walking toward her as she spoke, and he slipped a free finger into the top of her towel and pulled her to him. It was either follow or go naked. "Tink, peanut, goddess, pain in the ass—"

"Hey." She scowled.

Laughing, Max shook his head. "*Cassie,* my love, I was simply scared as hell. Not freed from the box's fiendish embrace. You never listen to me and I wanted to make sure that you knew I meant business. I was just using your name for emphasis. Of course, that backfired on me, too." Then Max sighed. "Not to mention I had some personal issues going on after hearing Victor's revelations."

Cassie narrowed her eyes at the memory of Victor's enjoyment as he tauntingly revealed secret after secret to Max. "Why do you think I racked him? He was such a turd." Cassie's hand flew to her mouth. "Oh, my gosh. What happened with Ivan? Did he take the treasure? Did—"

"I can practically see the wheels turning in your head. Ivan and I came to an agreement. If I say nothing and pretty much stay out of Russia for the rest of my life, I get to live. He got Stasi's diary, the treasure and what was left of Rajko's box, and I got Victor out of my hair. Forever." And what gorgeous hair it was, the light from the overhead chandelier bathing him golden like some pagan god come to life.

"Er, is Victor permanently…?"

"The FSS decided to crack down on his business conduct in their fair country. He's facing a number of charges that will make his stay in Russia's prison system a lifetime retirement. Trying to blackmail the FSS really pisses them off."

"But what about—"

"Natalia's fine and dandy. No worse for wear. She says hi, and told me to give you this." He jiggled the new lover's box.

"Anastasia. Will they ever admit—"

"Nope. Never heard of her. And neither have you." He winked and a gush of heat throbbed between her legs. "But, between you and me, I was able to get a few things of my own. We just can't ever tell anyone about them."

Max smiled devilishly. He slipped a hand into his pocket, then held out a yellowed piece of paper to Cassie.

She tilted her head. "But you kept going on about how dangerous Ivan was. You mean you stole something from him?"

He shrugged. "Well, he wasn't much of a threat to a tough broad like you. I mean, you got the drop on him at Victor's. Then at the Gypsy camp Ivan was running your basic enemy-at-gunpoint scenario and you whumped the bejesus out of his enemy's testicles. Bye-bye leverage, hello chaos. You created such a good diversion—I think I could've dug a hole and buried the treasure before Victor stopped bawling like a castrated calf. Let's just say that I had time to liberate a few things. I was telling Ivan the truth, though. We need to keep this between us."

Cassie nodded, fine with that, then slowly opened the folded paper. After a minute, her jaw dropped. "I knew it, I knew it was Anastasia. Where did you get this?"

The letter was from Anastasia to Rajko, written soon

after her recovery. In it, she expressed her thanks for his rescue and care for her injuries. She stated that she was giving her jewels to Rajko as a reward and because she had no need for them now that she was safe with the Gypsies and their king. Then she wrote of her love for Rajko, signing the letter with her name and royal title....

Cassie gaped at Max, who said, "The letter was slipped between two layers of wood inside the lid. The jewels were dug into snug little pockets, packed tightly so there was no rattling or shaking. You lucked out, Tink. There would have been no way to get them free without destroying the box. I guess that was Rajko's whole point when he made it—one could choose pleasure or treasure, not both."

"Is that what you really think?" Cassie asked.

"Well, Natalia said that the love letter was really the focal point for the charm. It grounds the magic." He shrugged, baffled. "Don't ask me. Apparently spells work better with a focal point. Strong emotion. So that's why the letter was inside the layers of wood. As for the jewels..." Max lifted a shoulder. "I think he was keeping them safe until he died. Back then, a person could go at any time. Stasi would have had to destroy the box to get the jewels, so Rajko could be sure her sexual needs would not be met by any other man."

Cassie shook her head, barely able to comprehend. "What's inside the new one?"

Max's mouth slowly curved into a cat-that-ate-the-canary smile. "Your old diary pages, plus a letter from me to you. You'll have to smash it to read it, but I'll give you a few hints…" Cassie wanted to pinch herself to see if she was back in one of her horrible, wonderful dreams.

"Hey, there's another present for you. You haven't even noticed it yet and it's the most important one."

Her gaze immediately lowered to the fly of his pants and he quirked an eyebrow and said, "Not that, short-stuff, he's already yours."

Then he lifted the lid of the box. Inside was an array of dazzling colors. "But you said—" Cassie tilted her head. She felt fuzzy and confused, as if she were listening to him talk underwater.

"I said I was able to get a few things. It's all part of the secret." Max plucked one of the glittering stones from the open box. He slipped something on to her finger, then nodded toward it. "Come on, peanut, don't argue. You can bust my chops later."

Her hand shook as she lifted her fingers and the huge emerald adorning the third finger of her left hand practically blinded her. Then it was like trying to *see* underwater because her vision blurred with her tears.

"Oh, Max, it's beautiful. But how did you get the stones?"

"You didn't think I really handed over all the jewels to Ivan, now did you?"

He reached over and put the new box on a nearby table. Then he plucked free the knot at the front of her towel. As the damp fabric slipped to pool at her ankles, he groaned. He slowly shook his head, his voice husky and rough when he spoke. "God, Tink. I love you like you can't believe. Now say yes, that you'll make me crazy every day for the rest of my life. You have no idea how much I miss making your fantasies come true."

Her pulse raced. The ultimate fantasy of her heart *had* come true—Max loved her and wanted to be with her even without the magical influence of the lover's box. And for the first time since they'd met, Cassie did exactly what he said. Throwing herself into his arms, she gasped, "I love you, too, Max. Always. No matter what."

Epilogue

MINERVA PARKER didn't think Max and Cassie would ever leave. For heaven's sake. As adorable as the young pups were, she would occasionally like to enjoy her own home. Besides, those two needed to get to France and start tracking down Cleopatra's coin.

It was pitiful, but if she wanted anything done right, Minerva had to do it herself. First she'd had to steal the lover's box. Then she'd had to stir things up with the Cleopatra's coin. But really, it was the ideal hunt. Cassie could get her feet wet and Max could easily breeze along the relic's trail. So they would have ample time for…other things.

A few minutes later Minerva found herself wondering when the right time would be for Cassie and Max to start having children. Hmm… She wasn't getting any younger….

* * * * *

The Colton family is back!
Enjoy a sneak preview of
COLTON'S SECRET SERVICE by Marie Ferrarella,
part of THE COLTONS: FAMILY FIRST *miniseries.*

Available from Silhouette Romantic Suspense
in September 2008.

He cautioned himself to be leery. He was human and he'd been conned before. But never by anyone nearly so attractive. Never by anyone he'd felt so attracted to.

In her defense, Nick supposed that Georgie could actually be telling him the truth. That she was a victim in all this. He had his people back in California checking her out, to make sure she was who she said she was and had, as she claimed, not even been near a computer but on the road these last few months that the threats had been made.

In the meantime, he was doing his own checking out. Up close and exceedingly personal. So personal he could feel his blood stirring.

It had been a long time since he'd thought of himself as anything other than a law enforcement agent of one type or other. But Georgeann Grady made him remember that beneath the oaths he had taken and his devotion to duty, there beat the heart of a man.

A man who'd been far too long without the touch of a woman.

He watched as the light from the fireplace caressed the outline of Georgie's small, trim, jean-clad body as she moved about the rustic living room that could have easily come off the set of a Hollywood Western. Except that it was genuine.

As genuine as she claimed to be?

Something inside of him hoped so.

He wasn't supposed to be taking sides. His only interest in being here was to guarantee Senator Joe Colton's safety as the latter continued to make his bid for the presidency. Everything else was supposed to be secondary, but, Nick had to silently admit, that was just a wee bit hard to remember right now.

Earlier, before she'd put her precocious handful of a daughter to bed, Georgie had fed his appetite by whipping up some kind of a delicious concoction out of the vegetables she'd pulled from her garden. Vegetables that, by all rights, should have been withered and dried. She'd mentioned that a friend came by on occasion to weed and tend it. Still, it surprised him that somehow she'd managed to make something mouthwatering out of it.

Almost as mouthwatering as she looked to him right at this moment.

Again, he was reminded of the appetite that hadn't been fed, hadn't been satisfied.

And wasn't going to be, Nick sternly told himself. At least not now. Maybe later, when things took on a more definite shape and all the questions in his head were answered to his satisfaction, there would be time to explore this feeling. This woman. But not now.

Damn it.

"Sorry about the lack of light," Georgie said, breaking into his train of thought as she turned around to face him. If she noticed the way he was looking at her, she gave no indication. "But I don't see a point in paying for electricity if I'm not going to be here. Besides, Emmie really enjoys camping out. She likes roughing it."

"And you?" Nick asked, moving closer to her, so close that a whisper would have trouble fitting in. "What do you like?"

The very breath stopped in Georgie's throat as she looked up at him.

"I think you've got a fair shot of guessing that one," she told him softly.

* * * * *

*Be sure to look for COLTON'S SECRET SERVICE
and the other following titles from*
THE COLTONS: FAMILY FIRST *miniseries:*
RANCHER'S REDEMPTION by Beth Cornelison
*THE SHERIFF'S AMNESIAC BRIDE
by Linda Conrad*
SOLDIER'S SECRET CHILD by Caridad Piñeiro
BABY'S WATCH by Justine Davis
A HERO OF HER OWN by Carla Cassidy

Romantic
SUSPENSE

**Sparked by Danger,
Fueled by Passion.**

The Coltons Are Back!

Marie Ferrarella
Colton's Secret Service

The Coltons: Family First

On a mission to protect a senator, Secret Service agent
Nick Sheffield tracks down a threatening message only
to discover Georgie Gradie Colton, a rodeo-riding single
mom, who insists on her innocence. Nick is instantly
taken with the feisty redhead, but vows not to let his
feelings interfere with his mission. Now he must figure
out if this woman is conning him or if he can trust her
and the passion they share....

Available September wherever books are sold.

Look for upcoming Colton titles
from Silhouette Romantic Suspense:

RANCHER'S REDEMPTION by Beth Cornelison, Available October
THE SHERIFF'S AMNESIAC BRIDE by Linda Conrad, Available November
SOLDIER'S SECRET CHILD by Caridad Piñeiro, Available December
BABY'S WATCH by Justine Davis, Available January 2009
A HERO OF HER OWN by Carla Cassidy, Available February 2009

Visit Silhouette Books at www.eHarlequin.com   SRS27598